Happily
Never After

An Anthology from Fey Publishing

Happily Never After
First Edition, June 2014
ISBN: 978-0692237649
Published by Fey Publishing
http://www.feypublishing.com/

Table Of Contents

The Law Of Mirrors

by Christina Elaine Collins

Milla hasn't let me go outside all morning. All this preparation for the visitors.

She turns on the faucet, and the water comes spurting out: cold. I shiver. The thought of visitors irritates me, though I'm told I should be excited this time. The daughter of the Russian diplomat is my age. My mother mentioned this fact as if it would make a difference, as if it would make the formalities less boring. Maybe it will. Maybe it won't. It all depends on what the diplomat's daughter is like.

I wonder if she'll want to go outside.

Milla wets the sponge and scrubs my arms. "Now turn a bit, so I can get your back."

I twist, and the drain holes chafe my skin, pressing a hundred tiny circles into my buttocks and the backs of my legs. "Ouch," I groan.

"Careful." Milla winces.

"Would it kill anyone to make tubs more comfortable?"

"Yes, actually." She smirks, lifts my hair, and scrubs my shoulders and neck.

"What?"

"Tubs weren't always like this, you know. They used to have just one small drain at the front, and a plug."

"Why?"

"So water could collect."

I laugh. I like when she tells jokes about the old days.

"It's true." She keeps scrubbing, her face serious. "Course, if anyone tried to build one of the old tubs now, they'd—you know—"

She pauses to slide a finger across her throat.

She lifts my arms and washes underneath. It tickles and I squeal, pulling away. Milla smirks again and adjusts the faucet; the water warms up. She leans in to scrub behind my ears, her face close to mine. Her eyes close to mine. I catch a glimpse of something in them, a tiny face, one in each, barely there, barely detectable. I blink and look away. I wonder if Milla noticed. Moments like these happen now and then. Everyone knows it, and no one mentions it.

Milla rinses my hair and pulls me to my feet, drying me with a towel. She dresses me, braids my hair, and escorts me down the hall, to where my mother and the visitors wait in the parlor.

My mother turns. "Ah, here she is—fashionably late. This is my daughter Elayne."

A man with a sour expression—the Russian diplomat, I assume —rises and bows. "A pleasure. And this is my daughter Dasha. She's come for the trip. Has never left Russia, so I thought it was time." His English is clean; I'm surprised. Past diplomats have needed translators.

The girl beside him, also wearing a sour expression, curtsies. I curtsy back.

"Elayne will be your host this week." My mother smiles at Dasha, who doesn't smile back. She turns to me. "Can you keep her company until dinner? We have matters to discuss."

I nod—not that I have a choice. My mother and the diplomat leave, talking rapidly about something to do with peace treaties, and Dasha and I stare at each other.

"Want to go outside?" I say.

"In this weather? I'd rather not."

"Oh. Is it raining?" I forgot she just came from outside. From inside, of course, there is no way of knowing if it's clear or gray, night or day.

"No. Too sunny. Bad for my complexion. But we can sit by a window if you want."

Window. I frown. I've heard that word before.

It was Milla who said it. During one of her bath stories. There used to be a thing called windows, she told me. Clear things that let you see outdoors while you are indoors. But they have long been banned—at least in this country. They must be legal in Russia.

Before I can tell Dasha we don't have windows, she pats her hair. "Can I use your mirror?"

"What?"

"Can I use your mirror? I need to fix my hair."

I stare at her.

She frowns. "Isn't that the right word in English? Mirror? Looking glass? *Zerkalo*?"

Is she mocking me? Or does she really not know? She couldn't have made it all the way to the capital without knowing, surely. "I don't have one," I say.

"No mirror? A pretty girl like you?"

"Pretty? What's that?"

She laughs. "Well, aren't you the modest one."

I consider asking for clarification, but decide it's not worth it. Probably some Russian lingo that doesn't translate.

"Can I use someone else's mirror then?"

"No one else has one."

She frowns again. "No one in the whole palace?"

"No one in the whole country. At least, no one's supposed to."

She snorts. "Sure."

"What's funny?"

She stares at me. Her smile fades.

So she really doesn't know.

This isn't the first time this has happened. My mother has had other foreigners visit and forgotten to explain the law. Many countries know about it by now, but there are always the occasional visitors who don't. The ones who didn't pay attention when they crossed the border. The ones who didn't realize that the border patrols were looking for more than weapons when they searched their luggage. The ones who didn't connect the dots, when the guards asked if they had any glass. Metals. Water. Pots. Buckets.

"No mirrors," I say quickly. I feel a surge of guilt for using the word. "I guess no one told you. All specular surfaces are banned. So is anything that collects water. And portrait painting."

She blinks at me, then shakes her head. "Sure. Fine." She sighs, as if I'm a child telling lies and arguing with a child is not worth her time. "How do I look, then? How's my hair?"

"Sssshh!" I look over my shoulder. We're the only people in the room, but you can never know who's listening through walls.

"What's wrong?"

"That's treason."

She stares at me again.

"Showing any interest in your appearance is punishable by death," I say.

"Are you joking?"

"No.

"But why? I don't understand. Why can't people see their reflections?"

I shrug. "It's been like that since before I was born."

"You mean you don't know *why* it's been like that?"

I sniff. "Of course I know why."

But when I try to think of the specific reasons, I draw a blank. No one has ever asked me before. And perhaps no one has ever told me before. "It's bad for you," I say at last. I know that, at least.

"Why?"

Does she know any other word? "It just is."

She runs a hand through her hair. "Are you saying I won't be able to see myself at all while I'm here?"

"Yes. I suppose that's what I'm saying."

She stands up. "But I'm here for a week."

I shrug. "I've done it for fourteen years. Nearly fifteen."

Her eyes widen. I try not to look into them. "You mean you've never...seen yourself?"

"No." I don't count the tiny shape I've glimpsed in Milla's pupils.

"But don't you ever wonder..."

I flash her a look of warning.

"Haven't you ever been curious?"

I stand up. "I could report you."

She holds up her hands. "Fine. I'm sorry. It just doesn't seem fair—I'm not even a citizen. I shouldn't be subject to this. I do wish there was something I could look at, even a hand mirror..."

I watch her scramble around the parlor, peering at every surface. None of them will reflect, of course, but maybe she thinks our system isn't thorough. Her forehead shines. Is she sweating? As I watch her panic, I'm glad I'm not dependent on something the way she is, so dependent I can't go a day without it. My mother must have known what she was doing when she made that law.

I also wonder if there's something I'm missing out on.

I turn from this last thought, the way I turn from that tiny face in Milla's pupils.

When Milla finally comes to retrieve us for dinner, I follow her happily. Dasha follows me, unhappily. As we walk, Milla tries to fill the silence by giving Dasha a tour, pointing out this room and that painting. Dasha nods with insincere politeness. By the time we get to the east wing, Milla gives up on her tour-guide efforts.

A noise fills the wing. Milla waves at us to keep walking, but I turn to look. I can never resist. I peek around the corner, at the men dragging a woman across the floor. She screams and twists and kicks, but the men are twice her size. They are pulling her toward the stairs. That can only mean one thing.

"Where are they taking her?" Dasha says.

"The lower prison hall," I say.

"What did she do?"

4

"She's been caught with one."

Her face pales. She doesn't ask for further explanation; she must be catching on.

The woman looks a few years older than me. She has yellow locks that curl at the end, lips painted a deep red that I can see all the way over here, and a dress suggestive of a merchant or doctor's wife. I wonder what she wanted with a mirror. It amazes me how some still get through. Smuggled through the border, or hidden under floorboards until the coast seems clear. But those people never get away with it for long. Not with my mother in charge. And not with her generous rewards for reporting mirror criminals.

"What are they going to do to her?" This time Dasha whispers.

"Hang her, obviously."

She pales even more, so I decide not to go into the details. Like how they'll pin back the woman's eyelids and force her to watch her execution in the same mirror she's been caught with. I've never actually seen a hanging—I'm not allowed to attend, they're meant for the villagers—but I hear they're fascinating. And effective.

This woman knows it's going to happen to her. Her screams claw at my ears. I watch the guards take her through the doors and wonder, like I always do, what drove her to mirrors—to madness, as my mother says. It occurs to me that Dasha might know the answer. I glance sideways at her, but Milla ushers us along and I don't ask.

"Have you ever been down there?" Dasha mutters as we walk.

"Where?"

"The lower prison hall."

"No. My mother won't allow it."

She doesn't say anything else, and we continue in silence. I don't tell her that the lower prison hall is only for mirror criminals. That we have a second unit, the upper prison hall, for people caught with other specular surfaces—buckets of water, materials like glass and silver, things harder to prove as having criminal intent. Those people receive a lesser sentence, only a lifetime in prison. It's trickiest with cases involving water because the suspect can dump the evidence in the dirt, but my mother always makes sure there is hard proof before sentencing someone. She's much fairer than her stepmother was, they say. And in more ways than one, others joke, though I don't get the joke—perhaps because I never knew my stepgrandmother.

oooooo

I haven't been the best host to Dasha this week.

5

As she and her father prepare to leave, she doesn't seem at all sad. Milla and I watch their carriage depart. Dasha doesn't stick her head out the window to look back or wave. She probably can't wait to get back to her mirrors.

Until a week ago, Dasha was like me, never having left her home country. I consider how I would have answered if she and I had become friends this week and she'd asked me to go with her to Russia and stay in their imperial palace with nesting dolls and Rublev paintings. And windows. And baths that have only one drain hole.

And mirrors.

There is no point in wondering, because we're not friends. The carriage disappears around the bend. I look away, at the impenetrable wall in the distance, closing off what had once been the palace lake, according to Milla. Or what is still the palace lake, I suppose. Who knows what's left behind there.

Milla sighs—I think she fancied the Russian diplomat—and turns to me. "Time for lessons, then."

I groan, following her inside. "But I worked all through lunch yesterday. Do they study this much in Russia?" It's the first country that comes to mind.

Milla raises an eyebrow. "Are you being ungrateful again?"

"No."

"Our society's considered the most intellectual in the world. You should be proud."

"I am." I realize my mistake. She'll go off on one of her rants now.

"Be thankful. Your mother's made us better, forced us to focus on our insides. Saved us from vanity, envy, superficiality. Self-consciousness. Insecurity."

"I know, I know." I've heard it all before. I realize now that this is what I should have told Dasha, when she asked why we have the law. But these things are like the alphabet, and you never think to explain the alphabet to anyone. My mother is so good, so principled, that most people can't stop talking about her. Milla is one of those people—maybe even her most adamant follower—going on and on about her goodness and wisdom. There are, of course, the few who don't like my mother, but I don't hear much about them. I mostly hear about all the good she's done for humanity, but I'd rather hear these things from my mother herself. Teatime on Mondays is when I get to see her—the best part of the week—and that's today; I'm already impatient. I had to miss last week because of Dasha.

"She's also made us more productive." Milla is still going on. "Less time grooming in front of the mirror. Did you know, before her intervention, the average woman looked in the mirror eight times a day? Some even admitted to seventy. Seventy! And men weren't far behind. Can you believe how much time we used to waste on our reflections?"

I nod and point out that she has spinach in her teeth.

When we get to the study room, Milla makes me solve pages of equations. I stare at the numbers and symbols, but they blur together. I look over at her as she flips through a book.

"Have you ever looked in one?" The words come out quiet.

"In what?" She licks her finger and turns a page. She always licks her finger, even when the pages aren't stuck together.

"You know."

She looks up. I wait for her to scold me, to tell me I should never talk like that. She looks at the wall. "Yes." She blinks. "I mean, before the law of course. Remember, I'm much older than you, older than your mother, even. I was around before the law. And that's how long it's been since I've—" She shakes her head. "I'm grateful. I was young then, and now—" She laughs, but not her usual, cheerful laugh. "Why would we want to watch ourselves grow old? Why would we want to see that? We're being kinder to ourselves this way. Your mother's being kinder to us."

oooooo

The servants set up the drinking tubes in front of us.

I lift the tube to my mouth and sip my tea, black, just as I like it. My mother lifts hers and we sip together. I treasure this hour, just me and her, because she is so busy the rest of the week. She tells me all kinds of things about politics and geography and asks me what I'm learning in lessons. It's my favorite day.

The servants bring in a rolling cart with tarts, biscuits, and fruits—pears, bananas, oranges, and some red, round fruit I've never seen before.

One of the attendants gasps. "How did these get in here?" he hisses at the other.

The second attendant's face turns the same color as the strange fruit. "I—I'm sorry—I didn't see them. There's a new chef. He must not have been told—"

"How could you forget to tell him? Consider yourself dismissed."

"It's all right." My mother waves a hand. "It's been, what, fifteen years? I think I can manage the sight of an apple."

An apple...the stories...they say my mother almost died because of an apple.

"I'm *most* embarrassed, Your Majesty. We don't want you to

have to think about it—you don't need any reminders."

We watch the servants scurry out of the room with the cart.

I sip my tea and ask, as casually as I can, "Why'd she try to kill you?"

She looks at me. "Why does it matter?"

"Aren't you tired of my asking?"

She sighs. "Because I was prettier than her."

My mind jumps to something Dasha had said, a word with a similar sound. "What does that mean—prettier?" I say, again as casually as I can.

"Ah." She grimaces and presses her palm to her forehead. "I forget myself sometimes, when I'm in private. That's an old word, from the time before. But I figure I can trust you not to repeat it."

"I won't," I say. "What does it mean?"

She bites her lip. "I might as well explain. When you take my place someday, you'll need to know why things are the way they are."

Take her place? The thought makes my leg bounce. And my palms sweat.

"All right." She folds her hands. "You know how when you look at people, and some are nicer to look at than others? Easier on the eyes?"

"Yes. I think so."

"Those people are prettier. That's what pretty means."

I laugh. "That's it? She tried to kill you because of that?"

"To her it was enough. It was enough that I was prettier."

"Says who?"

"What?"

"Prettier says who?"

She blinks at me. Maybe I shouldn't have asked.

A grin breaks across her lips. She reaches over and strokes one of my curls. "See, that's how I know you're my daughter. Your father would be proud—rest his soul. You ask the questions I used to ask, the ones that sparked the law in the first place. That's why we have the law. So that what happened to me never happens again. So that no one will suffer the fate I almost suffered, at the hands of someone mirror-obsessed." She laughs and shrugs. "Sure, it was dumb of me—opening the door, letting her in, taking the apple. But what my stepmother really did—it had nothing to do with the apple. What my stepmother really did was worse than trying to kill me."

I frown. "What could be worse that that?"

"She condemned me to be known for my beauty alone. She made it the only thing I had. So that even if the apple didn't work, even if I lived, one day I'd grow old and wrinkled like her, and have nothing."

"Beauty?"

"Sorry. Another word from the old days."

"Oh."

"Listen." She leans forward. "Want to know the true law of mirrors? Once you look in one, you'll want to look again. And again. Mirrors are unnecessary. And destructive. We're better off without them. This way, we can't agonize over our faces. We can't compare them to others'. Everyone is happier for it." The urgency in her voice impresses me. I decide that if I can ever be as passionate about something as she is about this, I'll consider myself a success.

oooooo

There is blood on my dress. I call for Milla. She gasps, then squeals, then helps me wash and change into a clean gown. "We should go tell your mother." She beams. "She'll be pleased to know you're a woman now."

"Maybe she'll be pleased, but I'm not. This is disgusting."

It's Wednesday, so my mother is doing her weekly audiences. Lately, though, it's been slow, and even if it's not, Milla says my mother will be glad we interrupted when she hears my news.

When we reach the doorway to the throne room, Milla holds out an arm, stopping me, and cranes her neck. I do the same. There's a woman having an audience with my mother—a young-ish woman, twenty-something, wearing a peasant's dress. She stands before my mother, fists clenched.

My mother sits in her chair leaning on her elbow. "Go ahead."

The peasant woman clears her throat. "There's a flaw in your system."

"Excuse me?"

The guards draw their weapons and step forward, but my mother holds up a hand. "Wait." She looks at the woman, challenging her. "Let's hear what she has to say."

The woman hesitates, as if surprised to have my mother's full attention. She stammers. "Maybe it's true that we can't compare our faces to others, but others still compare us to others."

"I'm not following you."

"My husband is having an affair. I found him—with a younger woman—"

"I'm sorry to hear that."

"This might have been prevented. If I could just use a mirror—if I could know how to look more desirable to him—then maybe—"

The guards again lift their weapons, and my mother again holds up her hand. "I'm afraid there's nothing I can do about such affairs. The law can only do so much."

"Why have it, then, if it's not going to succeed completely?"

"You can't deny we are better off than we were before."

"Are we?"

There is a moment of silence.

"Don't you see what the law's done to us?" The woman's voice rises. "A life without mirrors is a life of anxiety. Because we can see everyone else, we'll always wonder what they see. Mirrors are a relief in that sense."

"I'm afraid I don't agree with you."

The peasant woman shakes her head. "It hasn't made us deeper at all. We look in each other's eyes more often, but only to see our own reflections. That's what the law has done to us."

My mother blinks, then waves a hand. "Take her away."

The men come forward, seizing the woman. Her eyes widen. "No—wait." They cuff her, and I hear the panic in her voice. "I didn't do anything wrong. I gave my opinion is all—I—"

The men drag the shrieking woman away, as my mother sits massaging her temples. They seem to be pulling the woman east toward the stairs, the ones leading to the lower prison hall. But that can't be right. Surely they won't put her there—she doesn't even have a mirror.

Her cries fade to a distant wail.

"Perhaps now is not a good time," Milla whispers, and tugs me back down the hall.

oooooo

They've been happening more often lately. More arrests. More hangings. Milla keeps talking about them with the other attendants, as if I can't hear. Just this morning, one man was caught with a mirror sliver, the first man in a while; it's usually women. They say he was shaving his own face when the mirror magistrates found him. He claimed, when questioned, that his wife always nicked him when she shaved him and he wanted to do it himself, only he couldn't without a mirror.

And yesterday, my mother received tips that two women, from opposite sides of the country, may be in possession of full-length mirrors. Full-length! It turns out the tips were true.

And in the past week, seventeen arrests have been made on suspicion of treason alone. The upper and lower prison halls are growing crowded.

I look at my hands as Milla brushes my hair and does it up in a bun. "Why are there so many arrests all of a sudden?"

Milla shakes her head. "Beyond me. Nothing to worry about, I'm sure. Sometimes there are lulls, and sometimes there are bursts of unrest."

I stand up so Milla can dress me. I have a new gown—my chest area seems to have outgrown my other dresses—and Milla helps me slip it on. She stands back and looks at me.

"Oh," she says.

"What?"

She blinks. "Nothing—just—thought you were your mother for a second. Now you better move along. Don't keep her waiting."

I nod and hurry off to the parlor for Monday teatime. I'm anxious to speak to my mother. Milla doesn't know why the arrests are so frequent, but perhaps my mother has an idea. I also never told her my womanly news; there never seemed to be a good time, after that first day. Maybe today is the day.

When I enter the tearoom, she's bent over the table writing. "Have a seat," she says without looking up. "Let me just finish this letter. It's urgent."

"What about?"

Her pen moves furiously. I'm impressed she can still manage neat handwriting and talk at the same time. "Just alerting the Russian diplomat of our situation."

"What situation?"

"Oh, probably a false alarm..." She flips over the paper and continues writing on the reverse side. "We think a woman who had an audience with me last week may have been leading a rebel group. Now that she's been hanged, we suspect her followers may be planning an uprising."

Her pen makes a final flourish—her signature. She rings the bell on the table, and a servant appears. She hands him the letter. "It's ready to post."

He nods and retreats. She sighs and finally looks across the table at me. "Well, now, let's have some tea, shall—"

I wait for her to finish.

She blinks, her eyes fixed somewhere on my face. "You look b —" Her mouth freezes, a B on her lips.

"What? I look what?"

Her eyelids flutter. She looks away and shakes her head, like I've done something to annoy her. "Never mind."

She sips her tea tube and asks how my lessons are going. I try to carry on the conversation like any other Monday. But I can't help noticing the glances she casts me for the rest of the hour. Glances just like that first one. I look b— Blue? Brown? Bruised? Bored? Burnt? I'll never know.

After tea I wander in the garden, counting the birds. Eventually I give up, deciding they are countless. I watch a pair of sparrows play in the dirt. I wonder where they go to take their baths. They must fly high over the walls that surround the lakes and ponds.

The sun casts my shadow; I see my silhouette dance along the ground. A thin silhouette, and perhaps a little awkward. This is the closest I've ever come to seeing my whole self, besides looking in Milla's eyes. And it's the closest I ever will come. I know my hands, my arms, my legs, my feet, my stomach...I know them well. But I've never seen my face. Everyone has seen it except me.

Haven't you ever been curious? Dasha's words echo in my ears.

I'll admit I never was—until my mother gave me that look. I want to know why. I want to know what she saw that made her look at me like that.

Just one glance, if I can find a mirror...that's all I want, just one glance, and I'll never wonder again. And if anyone can get away with it, it's me. The queen's daughter. She wouldn't put her own daughter to death. She'd tell me that it can't happen again, probably, that I can't use my paints or the library for a week, but she'd let it go. Isn't that the advantage of being the queen's daughter?

But where can I find a mirror in a land without mirrors?

It can't be completely without mirrors, if the criminal count is rising by the day. Where did all those people find one—those wretches now locked in cells below, waiting for their turn at the noose?

It's all I can think about. During lessons, during meals, during the time I'm supposed to be sleeping. I try not to let Milla see my distraction. I try to act as normal as possible. As I sit in the tub for my bath, she talks about how thrilled she is for spring to be here. I smile and say I agree. I don't mention that the spring butterflies are in my stomach rather than outside where they belong.

When she leans in to get behind my ears, something happens— my hands reach up and grab her shoulders and hold her fast. As I hold her there, I look in her eyes.

"Elayne! What are you—"

There isn't enough time. I look for the face, the tiny little flash of a face in her pupils, but Milla blinks and slaps me, breaking away.

I touch my cheek. She shrinks back. I am technically her superior. I could have her dismissed, and she knows it.

"I'm sorry—" She wrings her hands, and I can tell she's embarrassed. "You caught me off guard."

"Milla." I stare down at my legs. "What do I look like?"

"Pardon?"

"What color are my eyes? Is my nose like yours? Do I have freckles? Am I..." What was that word Dasha and my mother used? "Pretty?"

Milla drops the sponge and backs away. "Where did you learn that word?" She's shaking. I've never seen her shake.

She's not going to cooperate, I realize. "I'm sorry," I say. "I'm sorry. I'll never say it again. Come back—I'm ready to be dried."

She hesitates, then finally moves back to the tub. Probably because she has no choice—it's her job. But she doesn't say anything more. I wonder if I should be worried. I've always trusted Milla. But when it comes to the possibility of treason—when her life could be on the line because of me—I suppose trust only goes so far.

I need to go to my mother before Milla does, just in case. I'll talk to her today. Explain this misunderstanding. And maybe she'll explain to me why she's been looking at me funny. It's not Monday, not our designated day, but certainly she'll welcome a five-minute break from her duties. Certainly she'll have a few minutes for her daughter.

I'm not sure where she spends Tuesday afternoons, so I try her bedroom first. Empty. I try the parlor. Empty. The dining hall. Also empty. I go down the corridor to her study. I never visit my mother here. She doesn't like to be disturbed in her study, but today seems like an exception if there ever was one.

The door is ajar and I squint through the crack, but I can't tell if anyone is inside. I push the door open and step in. The room is a mess, the desk covered with papers and books. The shelves are packed with folders and more books. My mother isn't here.

I walk over to the desk and spin the globe; it slows and stops, Russia facing me. I scan the bookshelves—history books, dictionaries, atlases. I notice one folder with a spine labeled *Dictionary Amendments*. I pull it off the shelf. Inside are old documents, browned, curling, the first one dated fifteen years ago.

Removals

By order of the queen, all existing copies of the English dictionary must be burned, and the following words will be removed from the next edition: attractive, beauty, beautiful, gorgeous, handsome, hideous, pretty, ugly, unattractive, unsightly...

The list goes on. I stare at it, a whole inventory of words I've never heard, words that used to be part of the English language. Below the list, another category: *Modifications.*

By order of the queen, the dictionary listing for the adjective "fair /fe(ə)r/" will be modified to remove the following sub-definition: "pleasing to look at."

I put the folder back on the shelf and pull out another folder labeled *Decrees*. I flip through pages and pages of documents, stopping on one that catches my eye.

The Mirror Law

Vanity, insecurity, jealousy, and superficiality are counterproductive to the development of a humane and just society. Man's access to, and alarming dependence on, looking glasses has encouraged these characteristics. Some look in mirrors out of sheer vanity, others because they dislike the way they look and want to change it. But whatever the reason, staring at oneself in the mirror does more harm than good. For one thing, during prolonged bouts of staring, even healthy women and men eventually start to focus on their imperfections, whether these imperfections are actual or imagined. For another, this time spent in front of mirrors detracts from our society's productivity and could be spent on more valuable tasks.

The only way to unseat this dangerous trend is to eliminate our ability to scrutinize our physical appearances. Therefore, all mirrors are hereby banned. Existing mirrors must be turned in for obliteration immediately, or else they will be confiscated during a nation-wide household search to be held in the coming weeks.

I flip the page and find another document, dated a year later:

Amendment to the Mirror Law

In light of the fact that citizens have been finding ways "around" the mirror law, all surfaces that create specular reflection are hereby banned. This includes not only mirrors, but any materials that have the properties of a mirror, such as windows, glass, aluminum, silver, and polished stone. Water is of particular concern, and several measures will be taken countrywide: Bodies of water within our borders will be closed off; washroom facilities will be redesigned to prevent the collection of water; cups, bowls, pots, and other objects that collect liquid will be destroyed; drinking water and other beverages will be dispensed from and consumed directly through tubes.

The clock in the corner chimes. Tensing, I shove the folder back on the shelf.

As I turn to leave, I spot a door—not the door I came through, but another door attached to the study.

I walk—not tiptoe—tiptoeing would imply sneaking—toward it. I lean my ear against it, hearing nothing. I turn the knob. The door opens, revealing another room: a long hall with vaulted ceilings and a person standing at the far end. I recognize her, even from this distance.

My mother stands in front of something on the wall—I can't quite see from this angle—and talking to it. She's talking in a strange way. I should leave. I should slip back out, before she sees. I realize this at the same moment that her head turns toward me.

"Elayne—how'd you get in here?" Her voice booms across the hall.

I hesitate. What *is* that thing on the wall?

"This is my private space. You aren't allowed in here."

I take a step forward. "That...that thing on the wall..."

She doesn't look at it. "Nothing. It's nothing."

I can see the gold frame of it, the small oval shape, and something, a flash, like the flash I saw when looking in Milla's eyes, only bigger.

It can't be true. It can't be. And yet it must be what I think it is.

"You?" I croak. "You of all people..."

She glares at me. "Do you just go walking into rooms that aren't yours, without permission? You've trespassed. This is my private space."

The butterflies in my stomach rise to my chest, their wings beating fiercely. "You—you've been killing all those people, and yet, this whole time..."

"If you don't get out right now—"

"This whole time, you've been hiding one in here." I step back. "You're a hypocrite. A fraud."

My mother's face ices over and I notice just how white, just how snow-white, it is. I don't know this woman in front of me. I've never known her, it seems. Our Monday teatimes were only snippets of her. Veiled snippets.

She sighs. "You're a liability now, you realize. A risk. And I can't have that." She snaps her finger.

Two manservants appear, almost immediately, from around a corner. They appear to be in on her secret. My mother nods her head toward me.

As they move in and I note the distance between my end of the hall and theirs, I decide I have time to escape. I turn back to the door I came through. It's closed—I must have closed it behind me—so I reach for the doorknob. All I have to do is get of this room—that's the first thing—I'll think about the next steps after—finding Milla, or maybe there won't be time—running, getting far off the premises, boarding a boat, perhaps to Russia.

I twist my hand, but the knob doesn't twist with it. I yank on the handle, but it doesn't budge.

I feel the men seizing me. An image comes to mind: the image of a yellow-haired woman with red lips, screaming, pleading, being dragged toward the east stairs. It occurs to me that I may soon see the place they took her.

But these men are dragging me toward my mother, while she watches, the way she watched that woman, as if with pity. They shove me against a column and tie my wrists behind it. I kick, but they grab my ankles and bind them.

"Gag her too," my mother says. "She'll try to talk, and as her mother I can't let my emotions get to me. Not when it comes to liabilities." Her voice is flat now, and I can't tell if she's being sincere or sarcastic.

One of the attendants pulls out a piece of cloth. The butterfly wings beat, throb, thrash. "Stop." I jerk my face away. "Get off." One attendant grabs my chin while the other shoves the cloth between my teeth and ties the ends behind my head.

"You can go now." My mother dismisses the men with a wave. They nod and disappear into the folds of the hall. She stands several feet away, contemplating me. I look back at her. For the first time, I fear her. I realize this is because I didn't know her well enough to fear her before.

Behind her I glimpse the gold frame, but her body blocks the rest from view.

"It's not the same one, of course," she says, admiring, or pretending to admire, her fingernails. "Not the one my stepmother used. But I can't imagine it's much different. All mirrors are the same, in the end." She pulls something out of her skirts and holds it up. An apple, with a bite-size piece missing. "This apple is older than you, though you could never tell. No one knows I kept it. It got caught in my skirts. I found it there when I woke. I saved it to kill my stepmother. But I didn't need it in the end. As you know." She smiles at the air. I wonder if she's talking to me or the apple or the mirror. It isn't clear.

"I saw them one more time, you know. The dwarves. After I married your father. After you were born. I never told anyone."

She rubs the apple against her skirts, as if to polish it.

"When you came, you were healthy. Smiling. She'll be pretty too, everyone said. Like her mother was. I wondered when they started using the past tense. By then, my dresses were too small.

16

People had stopped coming to see the fairest in the land. Even your father visited my room less."

I yank at my manacles. Why is she telling me this? Why is she doing this?

"One day you were crying so much, I couldn't calm you. The nurses came and took you away, to pacify you. I left—slipped through the cracks in the palace. Headed toward the woods. I'd only done it once, but I still remembered the way. I found their cottage. I realized then that it was the only place I'd felt happy. But even the dwarves didn't treat me the way they used to. They were still kind, but not like they were before. They asked me to do housework again. In the good days I hadn't minded; I was pretty then. I'd had that, at least."

She turns the apple over in her hand. "So you see? I didn't make these laws because I was a good person, or a deep person. I wanted to convince myself that was why. But these lives we're born into, they're mirrors within mirrors within mirrors. One poisoned apple after another. A vicious cycle."

She walks up to me and pulls off the gag, holds the apple to my mouth, presses it to my lips. "That's why I must do this."

At once I realize what's happening. What she intends to do. I press my lips together, as tight as I can. The apple smells like dust under my nose. Its skin feels cold as she pushes it against my mouth. I twist, trying to scream, trying to free my hands. My wrists burn. Milla! Where are you, Milla? If only you could see your hero now, what she is about to do to her own daughter...

My eyes water. I won't swallow the apple. I won't.

I could take a bite, and then, when she unties my fake-dead body, spit it back in her face and run. But the contact alone might kill me. I don't know how these things work. I only know I can't let her win.

A tear appears in the corner of my mother's eye—drips down her cheek. "That's why I must remove myself from the cycle," she says.

Before I can blink, she pulls the apple away from me, toward her own mouth, and sinks her teeth into it.

I watch her fall to the ground.

The thing behind her is now in full view.

In it someone blinks at me, pale and open-mouthed and tied to a column. I don't yet know if this stranger is ugly or beautiful or whatever the olden words are. But it doesn't matter because my mother was right. The law of mirrors has already won: I can't look away.

About Christina Elaine Collins

Christina Elaine Collins is a Pushcart Prize-nominated fiction writer and an MFA candidate and teaching fellow at George Mason University. Her fiction can be found in various publications such as *Jabberwock Review, Weave Magazine,* and *Rose Red Review,* and she was named a finalist for Heavy Feather Review's 2013 Fiction Chapbook Contest (Issue 3.1). She is the assistant editor for *So to Speak: A Feminist Journal of Language and Art,* and has been a writer-in-residence at the Kimmel Harding Nelson Center for the Arts as well as the Art Commune program in Armenia.

Rat-a-tat-tat

by Adam Millard

Beware the woods, stay well away,
Nobody is safe, not night or day,
The world is ruin'd, we saw to that,
Beware the sound of the Rat-a-tat-tat

– Childhood Nursery Rhyme Circa 2047

"But I don't *want* to go," Isme said, her body wracking with sobs. She was, Paul realised as he glanced down at her brown dress, wearing remnants of their supper; soup and breadcrumbs peppered her collar. For a girl of twelve, she showed no signs of maturing.

"Look, Isme," he said, offering her a handkerchief. "If we don't go, I'm going to be the laughing stock. It's my only chance to *be* something. Kaleb and Godfrey are going, and they won't let me hear the end—"

"Then go *alone*," Isme interrupted. The way in which she wiped the tears from the corner of her eyes irritated her brother. Everything that she did irritated him. "I don't see why I have to go with you."

Paul hadn't expected her to understand. They seldom went anywhere together, and certainly never at night time. If the truth be told, he was too scared to go alone. Not that he believed any of the stupid stories about Top-Half; they were too ridiculous to pay any heed. But he believed in the bandits and the cannibals roaming the forest. Oh, he sure as *hell* believed in those.

"You're coming with me, Isme, or I'm telling Pa about that boy you've been kissing. What's his name?"

Isme's countenance changed so much in that second that you might have believed her to be two separate people. "No, please, you mustn't tell Pa about Adrian. He'll *kill* him."

Paul grinned, satisfied with himself for giving her no real option. "Then we leave tonight," he said, running a hand through his jet-black hair. "And don't think about backing out on me. Not unless you want to see Adrian pinned to that tree over there." He pointed across to where an old oak stretched up towards the liquid sky. Black lava-clouds drifted slowly along, nonchalantly, as if they had always been there, and for Isme and Paul, they had.

Later that night, when Pa was drunk on a barrel of home-brew and sleeping off the results, Paul packed a rucksack with essentials. He doubted anything would go wrong, but it didn't hurt to carry a few weapons, a box of candles, and some food. In the case of the latter, it wasn't much, but they would – if Paul had appraised the distance to the centre of the forest correctly – be back in time for breakfast. Pa would wake at some point in the mid-morning; Paul was certain that the potency of his father's moonshine, and the ridiculous amount he had imbibed, would render him unconscious until then.

Isme had spent the best part of an hour sobbing out in the barn. Paul wondered if she was ever going to grow up. Since the bandits slew their mother almost three years back, Isme had cried almost perpetually. Paul often speculated that Isme was the reason that their father chose to spend his time soused. By marinating himself in whatever ungodly concoction he could muster, Pa didn't have to listen to Isme's incessant whining. *If only*, Paul thought, *there was room at the bottom of that barrel for two...*

"Come on. And pack that crying in. Anyone would think you were six." Paul led her out of the barn and into the night, where a bitter chill met them.

There wasn't much difference between night and day, other than the temperature change. You could sometimes use a thermometer as a timepiece. Ten below meant early evening. Twenty below and you could place the time around midnight. Paul guessed it to be somewhere around ten-thirty, and it would get a helluva lot colder before they reached the forest's centre. The same oil-slick clouds coasted along overhead; beyond them, the erratic flickering of lightning, no longer accompanied by the rumble of thunder. There hadn't been as much as a growl from above for over five years, yet the lightning was a constant.

They were less than a quarter of a mile from the house when Isme began to complain. "It's too cold," she said. "Why are we doing this, Paul?"

"I've already told you," her brother replied. "If I am to be considered brave, and a *Wanderer*, like Kaleb and Godfrey, I have to make it to the clearing at the centre of the forest in the dead of the night."

"Stupid rules," Isme hissed. "Your little gang are going to get themselves slaughtered. If the bandits don't get them, Top-Half *will*."

Paul shuddered at the mention of His name. "Stop that nonsense right now," he said, glancing across his shoulder as gooseflesh began to rise on the nape of his neck. "He's a *myth*, Isme. Something overprotective parents tell their children to keep them ferreted away. Ma told you about Top-Half so you would spend the rest of your days living in fear. Yeah, you'd be safer never leaving the house, but what kind of life is *that*? If the bandits or the cannibals want to get us, they'll break in and take us. As simple as that."

As soon as the words passed his lips he wished he could take them back. Not because he could see the effect they had had on Isme, but because he had put the fear into himself.

"I'm sorry," he said. "Look, it's a nice night. Just you, me, and the trees. We'll be home when it starts to get warm again, and you can spend the rest of the week kissing Adrian next to the barn, safe in the knowledge that your secret will never reach Pa's ears."

Paul couldn't be certain – it was so dark now with the trees all around that it was a chore just to see where you were walking – but he thought he perceived a change upon his sister's face.

Almost a smile.

They walked through the woods, a jungle of long-dead trees and desiccated roots, in silence. Somewhere, off in the distance, creatures called to each other; their falsetto screeching should have terrified the young duo, but instead gave them something to focus upon as they traversed the trees.

"How long do you think we've been walking?" Isme asked. "Can we stop to rest for a while?"

Paul grinned. "Not long enough, and no," he said. "Honestly, Isme, I don't know how you've survived this long."

She thought back to before Ma died, to a time when Pa was always sober, taking care of them, keeping the bandits at bay with his machete, firing rounds – that was when there was still ammunition – at packs of cannibals as they attempted to breach the house. She'd survived because people had helped her, and now she was hopeless for it. With Ma dead and Pa practically pickled, she realised she could only count on Paul to keep her safe, to protect her from the evils of the Aftermath; the cannibals, the bandits, Top-Half...

"Here you go," Paul said, pulling her from her reverie. In

his hand he held a bottle of cloudy water and a chunk of bread. "Don't say I never give you anything." He smiled.

She took the food and ate, washed it down with the water. The fact that she couldn't see the bottom of the bottle due to the opaque liquid didn't stop her from gulping it down, thirstily. She felt better for it after.

"Are we good to get moving again?" Paul asked. He didn't know what time it was – nobody did anymore, not exactly – but he knew they would be cutting it mighty close.

Isme thanked him for the brief respite, and said, "Come on then, *Wanderer*. Let's go meet your Pack."

The rest of the journey was a lot more pleasant; Isme had ceased asking asinine questions, and Paul's own trepidation had been replaced with something much more agreeable: the knowledge that, after all these years, he was going to become a Wanderer.

Kaleb and Godfrey were among the greatest hunters the Aftermath had ever known; to place himself alongside them, battling bandits and providing the surrounding villages with meat and sustenance, was something he'd desired for years. They had three years on him, which would make him the youngest Wanderer in the Pack, no less skilled, and certainly no less feared. *If only Ma could see me now*, Paul opined.

As the forest gave way to a clearing, Isme relaxed, sliding down a tree as if she had partaken in some ancient Olympics. Paul began to scour the area for any signs to suggest that the Wanderers had been there. He found nothing, but knew this was the clearing at the centre of the woods, the place they had agreed to meet.

"Anything?" Isme asked, breathlessly.

Paul shook his head. "They'll be here. It's not cold enough to be midnight just yet. I think we made good time."

Through the trees, inkblot clouds were visible. The shrill *ca-caws* of mutated birds rang out all around, as if in dissension at the young siblings' presence. The brother and sister duo had known nothing else; since birth, the world had been filled with transmuted creatures; the birds had been possessed of a third wing; the wolves had extra appendages which hindered them more than anything. Sitting in the library, upon a dusty shelf, was a book filled with illustrations of what animals looked like before the Event, and to Paul they looked...well, *odd*. How could a bird fly with just two wings? What use was a cat with one head?

Just then, there came a sound that turned Isme's blood to mercury. A *rat-a-tat-tat* that she had been afraid of since birth. Ma read her the poem every night before bed, and she'd recited it religiously ever since.

"Did you hear that?" she said, her mouth open in a wide O. Paul thought she looked comical.

"Hear what?" he said, making his way towards the tree which she was pushing herself against, as if in hiding. "Isme, what did I tell you? Huh? No silliness."

Rat-a-tat-tat...

Her eyes bulged from their sockets; even in the impossible darkness, Paul could see that she was terrified. "You heard that, *right?*"

He had heard it; his own gooseflesh caused him to shudder. "Sounds like a bird pecking a tree," he said, more to alleviate his own fears.

"The world is ruin'd, we saw to that..."

"Isme, don't start with that stupid rhyme. I swear, if Ma could see you now she'd..."

Rat-a-tat-tat...

"Beware the sound of the Rat-a-tat-tat." As she finished the rhyme, her voice cracked and tears began to flow, streaming down her cheek, glistening with each flash of lightning the heavens provided. Paul was too angry to comfort her, and yet he knew that he should. It was his duty, and no-one else's.

He stepped close to her, draped his arms across her tiny, frail shoulders. "Isme, everything's fine. You're just frightening yourself. Top-Half doesn't exist; everybody knows that."

"What if he *does*?" she gasped. "What if the elders were right?"

"Well, they're *not*, and I forbid you to—"

Something broke to his left; he snapped his head across, his eyes adjusting quickly to the darkness that met his gaze. Enveloped by shadows, a figure stepped forward. As it entered the clearing, Paul pulled his sister into his chest. This was something not meant for her eyes.

Rat-a-tat-tat...

"I'm scared," she sobbed into Paul's chest. "Is it there? Is it Top-Half?"

"Shhhh," Paul said, stroking her lifeless hair with one sweaty palm. "Everything's okay."

The thing came closer. With each step it produced the same deathly rattle. *Rat-a-tat-tat...Rat-a-tat-tat*, for Top-Half was exactly that. A torso sat mounted on wooden stilts; the face atop the torso in a constant grimace, the melted features something from a terrible nightmare. The horrifying sound produced as it approached was resultant of its legs rubbing together; a grasshopper from the very bowels of Hell.

23

They had all heard the stories; they had all heard the rhyme about the man who had lived through the Event, despite being severed and mutilated, his body from the waist down replaced by wood.

Top-Half; a demon in a world of cannibals and bandits.

"I don't want to die," Isme sobbed. Paul could feel her tears penetrating the material of his shirt.

He shushed her once again, told her everything would be alright. As he closed his eyes, he saw their Pa, drunk and oblivious. Tomorrow he would wake to an empty house. Would he even *care*?

Rat-a-tat-tat...

Paul didn't think so. He kissed Isme atop her head, and listened as the tapping came closer, and closer.

Rat-a-tat-tat...

Rat-a-tat-tat...

Rat-a...

ABOUT ADAM MILLARD

Adam Millard is the author of thirteen novels and more than a hundred short stories, which can be found in various collections and anthologies. Probably best known for his post-apocalyptic fiction, Adam also writes fantasy/horror for children. He created the character *Peter Crombie, Teenage Zombie* just so he had something decent to read to his son at bedtime. Adam also writes Bizarro fiction for several publishers, who enjoy his tales of flesh-eating clown-beetles and rabies-infected derrieres so much that they keep printing them. His *Dead* series has been the filling in a Stephen King/Bram Stoker sandwich on Amazon's bestsellers chart, and the translation rights have recently sold to German publisher, Voodoo Press. When he's not writing about the nightmarish creatures battling for supremacy in his head, Adam writes for *This Is Horror*, whose columnists include Shaun Hutson, Simon Bestwick and Simon Marshall-Jones.

SmallMarg And The Star-Heart

by Jax Goss

The children called it the Thing. The adults, when they spoke of it at all, called it the Time. The children, as children do, spoke of it in whispers away from the ears of adults. They spoke of it like legend, folklore, history, truth.

The adults never spoke of it at all, unless they had to, and then with awkwardness and shame, as though by bringing it up, by naming it, they would bring it back.

The children played amongst its wreckage, the piles of metal, some still smoking though years had passed. Mountains of rubble with treasures in them. Treasures, you understand, for a child, for a child's idea of treasure is very different to a grown-up's.

She was the smallest of the Ones Who Played. Her legs were shorter than the others, and she spent much time asking them to slow down and wait up. They seldom listened; if she wanted to run with them, she had to learn to keep up. Her second oldest brother would sometimes wait for her, laughing, needling, encouraging her: "Come onnn."

She had short legs, and pigtails, and freckles across her nose. She got sunburnt too easily, too quickly – practically a sin since the Thing had come. There were stories of a substance that had stopped the sun from burning. The Layer of Oz One. But the Thing had burnt it up, or at least, enough of it that now there was no protection, and they ran fully covered, all their skin, their eyes, like tiny radioactive suits scampering and clambering around on the rubble.

With all the protection, she burnt anyway. She would come home, her skin red and peeling, and her mother would weep, and rub lotion into her, and beg her to stay inside like the Good Children did. She would promise solemnly to do so, for she hated to see her mother cry, but when the Ones Who Played would come calling for her brother, she would sneak out too, for the promise of treasure and adventure was too great to ignore.

It was overcast the day they found It. The Pilot. One boy, one of the oldest, tripped over a bar, and reached out his hand to catch himself, pressed against a button none of them had recognised as a button, and there was a hiss of air, a whoosh of depressurisation, and then, with a squealing of torn metal, the whole thing shook and moved and opened up.

They all drew back for a moment, glancing at each other, trying to gauge whether it was okay to be scared. She was too curious to be afraid. So she crept up to the hole and looked inside. In the midst of the wires and steel she could see a suit - humanoid, but definitely alien.

"H-hello?" she said to it.

One of the other girls laughed. "It's been decades, it won't still be a-..."

She was interrupted by a raucous noise. The other children all ran, scattering into the heaps of rubble. She stayed. Her curiosity was stronger than her fear. After a few moments, she recognised it as coughing, or something like it. There was a long silence. Then she heard a voice. It was speaking in another language, one she did not know.

She approached again. "Um. Hello? We don't... Do you speak English?"

"Engl-issss" the Pilot hissed. There was a long moment. Then the Pilot spoke again.

"Eearth. Planet 3 of System 569 in the Borath region. Inhabitants: Human. Primitive technology, no known galactical affiliates. Greetings."

"Hi. What's your name?"

"Identifier: Halimorphaxistenthorpogalmanstiyak 5."

She blinked. "May I call you Yak5? I am Margaret Susanna O'Flannagan-Hughes, but they call me SmallMarg."

"Designation acceptable."

She giggled then. "You talk funny."

The Pilot was silent for a second. "Do you mean to imply my speech patterns appear unorthodox? One moment."

There was some whirring and beeping.

"There, that should be better."

She nodded. "Yes, now you sound like a person."

"I am not a person. I am a star-rider. I crashed, and my systems went into stasis until you released me. I must make repairs before I can get home."

"You destroyed the whole world."

"I... what?"

She nodded. "They don't talk about it. But there were other things. People travelled through the air, and could talk to people on the other side of the world. They say hundreds of people would live in a single building. Now there are only a few hundred left, and no one remembers how to do those things any more. The grownups don't talk about it. But we know. When you came, the world ended, and only we were left."

There was a long sad, silence, and when the Pilot spoke again, there was something like grief in its voice. "I regret that deeply. Earth was on the cusp... I must have set you back so far. I can remedy some of it. The damage to the environment. I can restore the ozone, and the weather as I leave."

Weather. It was a thing of legend. Water that came from the sky, falling, free for anyone, instead of needing to be mined and siphoned from underground streams.

"I need something. Can you help me?"

She nodded, with the absolute assurance of a child.

"I'll need the star-heart of my vessel, which appears to be missing."

"Star-heart?"

"It will look like a jewel. A shining object."

"Ohh." She crouched. "It is Gone."

"Gone?"

She nodded. "Yes. The Mayor took it. It was very shiny, and beautiful, and he wanted it, so he took it."

"Can we get it back?"

"It is Gone."

"Gone where?"

She frowned. She did not understand what he meant. Everyone knew once something or someone was Gone, there was no *where*, there was no coming back from Gone. She stood up, and pointed to the big building on the horizon.

"You know. GONE."

"It is in the building?"

"The Mayor takes what he wants. And once it is Gone, it stays Gone. Like your star-heart. Like my father. Nothing comes back from Gone. Everyone knows that."

There was a pause. "I don't." There was something in the Pilot's voice, just for a second, something like determination and anger that made her pause.

"SmallMarg? I need you to be very brave for me. If you can do it, you will help your world. If I can get the star-heart back, I can restore your ozone and weather patterns. The sun will not be as poisonous as it is now. It will rain again. I am very sorry for the damage I did. I can't fix your society, but I can repair the environmental damage, which may help."

She nodded. "That would be nice."

"But you'll need to go into that building and bring me back my star-heart."

She shook her head. It was impossible.

"SmallMarg. This is not impossible. I will tell you how."

oooooo

She stood at the base of Gone and looked up. It went up forever into the sky. The Pilot had said that there were seven floors. She did not know how he had known that; no one who went into Gone ever came out, she knew that. He had also known the star-heart was on the seventh floor.

She was not sure that, if she went in, she would come out. She was afraid, of course, and she wished she had told her mother where she was going. But it was too late for that, and she couldn't refuse. If he was right, she could save the world. Bring back the Weather and the Oz One. She couldn't say no.

So she moved forward, and followed the building around the side. There were big open doors at the front, with an empty lobby inside. Sometimes the Ones Who Played would dare each other to run up to the doors, so they had all peeked inside and seen the large front desk, dusty and abandoned. But The Pilot had said not to go in the front doors. There was another on the side.

When she got there, she pushed gently on it, and it creaked open, just as The Pilot had said it would. He'd said something about how the "security system appears to be disarmed". She'd thought but not said that there was no need for security on a building everyone was too afraid to go near.

She slipped inside before she could think about what she was doing. It smelt like dust and abandonment. In front of her was a metal staircase leading up. Her footstep rung out on the first step, loud, too loud, and she froze, and waited for a million years to see if someone would come. Nothing continued to happen, so she slipped her shoes off, and began padding as quietly as she could up the stairs to the first landing.

Here the door to the next set of stairs was locked. The Pilot had said that might happen, and told her what to do. She peeked into the corridor, and saw a long row of abandoned doors. She wondered if there was anyone here. It seemed empty. The Pilot had said there would be another set of stairs somewhere, one without doors, that was more open and dangerous, but would "work in a pinch". She wasn't sure what a pinch was.

She took a deep breath and walked out into the horribly

29

exposed corridor. Silence roared in her ears, and she walked as quickly and quietly as she could along it, until she found the staircase he had said would be there. She walked up it as fast as she could, peeking out carefully onto the landing of the third floor as she did so.

She was just thinking that this was not as hard as she thought it would be when she heard a noise. It was a low mournful noise, a terrible, sad, heartbreaking noise, and she jumped back down the stairs a little at the sound. After a few moments, the noise continued, but nothing else happened, so she peeked around the stairwell and down the corridor. There was nothing to see.

She walked along it slowly, quietly, following the sound. It took her to a door. The door was closed, so she rested her ear against it, listening to the mournful sound with her eyes closed. It sounded like loneliness. It went on for a long time, and then stopped, suddenly. She heard the noise of someone standing up, and pushed away from the door, ready to run. She wasn't fast enough, and the door swung open, revealing a tiny old shrivelled man. He blinked at her for a moment, while she gaped at him in return.

"Who-" he began, in confusion.

"Please-" she said at the exact same moment.

They both stopped, and then the little man grabbed her arm, and pulled her inside, pulling the door shut behind her.

"Who are you?" he creaked at her, his voice old and unused. "What are you doing here? No one comes here."

"I'm SmallMarg," she replied. She was afraid now, afraid the man would tell the Mayor she was here, afraid he would hurt her, make it so she could never get the star-heart and go home.

He must have seen how afraid she was, because his face softened. His skin was frail, like paper, she thought he must be hundreds of years old. But when he smiled, his eyes smiled too, and made him a lot less scary.

"Don't be scared, child. It has just been so long since anyone came here. I thought there was no one left in the world. And then you walk in, as if it's nothing, and listen at my door. It is strange. Now tell me, why are you here?"

"I came for the star-heart." The words were out of her mouth before she could stop herself.

"The what?" the man asked.

She clapped a hand over her mouth. "I think it's meant to be a secret."

"A secret star-heart? What is a star-heart?"

She began to cry, sitting down in a chair nearby. She sobbed, her little shoulders shaking. "I've ruined everything now. I was supposed to come and get it and then the Pilot would fix everything and bring back the Weather, and now you've caught me, and you're going to make me be Gone too like everything else in here, and my mommy doesn't even know where I am and I've messed it all up."

The man looked shocked for a moment, as if he'd forgotten how to deal with someone else's emotions. Then he sat down beside her and patted her awkwardly on the shoulder.

"There, there. I am sure it is not as bad as all that. Let me help you. I have lived here for a long time. If what you are looking for is in this building, I am sure I can help."

SmallMarg sniffled and wiped her nose on her sleeve. She turned to him and said, "But, aren't you Gone too?"

"Gone?" The man was puzzled. "I don't know what you mean."

"Everyone knows. If you go into Gone you never come out."

"This building is Gone?"

SmallMarg nodded. The man frowned.

"Certainly, I don't go out any more, but that's because I thought everything was destroyed. I have a garden in one of the other rooms that supplies my needs. I've not been to the upper floors in a long time. The elevators don't work any more, and my legs are not what they once were."

"But what about the Mayor?"

"The Mayor?"

SmallMarg looked at the man like he was crazy. "Yes. He is in charge. When the Thing came, he took over, told everyone what to do. Everyone was grateful. But then he got mean, and started taking people, and they were Gone. And then he took things too – special things, things he liked. No one could stop him. All the things were Gone. They came here, and then never came back."

The man frowned for a moment, and then he laughed, suddenly. "Oh! You mean The General. Yes, he was a bit forceful. He lived on the seventh floor. He died, child. Many years ago. You mean people out there, they still fear him?"

She nodded. "The grownups don't talk about it, but we tell the stories. Everyone knows to stay away from Gone."

"This building?"

She nodded.

"Then why are you here?"

"Because, I..." she fell silent.

"Ah. It was a secret. Well let me see. You said something about a star-heart? I don't know what that is, but I would guess given what else you've told me that the General took something important, and now you've come to find it?"

She nodded.

"Well, if it's here it will be in his apartment. Seventh floor, number 6. He did like knick-knacks. I don't think any of them were particularly valuable though. Except maybe the things he used as tax during the Time. In any case, that's where it will be, this star-heart of yours. If it's here at all. I can't come up with you, but you should have no trouble getting it. Just be careful on floor six. There used to be something there. Some kind of animal I think. I haven't heard it in a while, but it may still be lurking about, living on rodents."

She stood. "Thank you for your help."

She started towards the door. Then she paused.

"What was the noise? The thing I heard?"

"This." He picked up a strange object and held it to his lips. The noise came out again.

"What is it?"

"A bassoon. I learnt to play it when I was very young. All the songs I remember are sad though. I suppose that's fitting. It may be the only working musical instrument in the world now."

She smiled. "I liked it."

As she walked towards the stairs, she heard the man's bassoon start up again.

oooooo

She climbed to the fourth and fifth floors with no accident, but as she approached the sixth, she remembered what the man had said, and began to get very nervous. She climbed the stairs slower and slower, but it didn't matter, she still reached the sixth floor before she felt ready for it.

She peered around the corner into the corridor. Everything seemed still and silent. She knew she should just hightail it up to the next floor as fast as possible, but she was very curious about this animal the bassoon-man had mentioned.

Maybe I'll just take a small walk, she thought, even as she knew that was crazy. Get the star-heart, get out. That was what she should do. She was congratulating herself on her sensible decision even as her feet carried her down the corridor. She listened for a moment at each door, but all was silent. Then, just as she was convincing herself that it was time to go, there was nothing here, she heard a whine. It was pitiful, and didn't sound dangerous, just sad and sore. It came from two doors down.

Part of her brain was screaming at her to leave, now, go up to the seventh floor, do what she came here for. But another part knew that if whatever-it-was was in pain or in trouble, she should help. So she opened the door.

Whatever-it-was was crouched under a table in the kitchen. It

32

was dark, and dust hung in the air. The thing growled a mewling painful growl. She could see matted fur, and two shining eyes. It took up the whole space beneath the table.

There were no more animals, not like this. There were stories about places where animals had been, before the Thing. People had kept them, in their homes, or in special places called Zoos. She'd once found a book with pictures, and had spent a long time poring over them.

This did not look like something that would have been kept in a home. This looked more like a Zoo Animal. She crouched. She did not know how you were supposed to deal with animals, so she treated it like she would a small hurt child.

"Hi. Are you okay?"

The thing growled again, but stayed where it was. It seemed more afraid than malevolent.

"Are you hurt? Hungry? What do you eat, I wonder?" She glanced around, but couldn't see anything. She remembered what the man had said about rodents. There were still rodents, of course. Rats and mice and sometimes shrews. She saw that there was a bowl in the sink, and the tap was dripping. She poured some water into it, and took it close to the animal. Leaving it close enough to tempt it, but far enough to not be threatening.

"Thirsty?"

The animal stared at her for a while, then unfolded and moved to the water, lapping it up. In the comparative light of the kitchen she could see its fur was matted, and its ribs stuck out like it was starving. This wasn't that unusual. Most people looked like that too these days. Somewhere under the muck though she could imagine it sleek and powerful.

"Poor thing. This doesn't seem like a good place for you. If I can find a way to help you, I will."

The animal stared at her as if it understood. Then it ran its tongue over its lips once. This made her realise that being the tastiest morsel in the room was probably not the best idea, so she retreated, closing the door behind her. She ran, then, up the stairs to the seventh floor. She didn't stop until she was standing at the door to apartment 6.

She took a deep breath and opened the door. This apartment was bigger than the ones she had seen already. Like the others, though, it was dusty.

It was also cluttered. Every corner, shelf and surface was covered with things. Candlesticks, snowglobes, small statues of kittens. There was a giant display board full of medals. There were hundreds of books. The bassoon-man had been right. The General sure had liked knick knacks.

She was just wondering how she was going to find the star-heart in here, when she saw it. In pride of place on the mantelpiece of a fake fireplace. It was large enough to fill her hand, it was beautiful, and it was glowing in the dim light. Not a lot, which was why she hadn't noticed it right away, but just enough. A small light in its heart, pulsing. Like it was sending out a signal, trying to attract attention.

Carefully, almost reverently, she picked it up. It was warm in her hands. She watched the light pulse for a moment, and then, suddenly aware of the importance of the thing she was holding, she turned and ran, out of the room, and down the stairs, flight after flight, with no more thought then to get it to the Pilot as soon as she could. She ran, out into the light, out of Gone, the first person, she believed, to ever come back, and back to where the Pilot was waiting.

oooooo

He told her she was very brave. Before he left, she asked him about Gone.

"We were all so scared of it, of what we thought was in there. But it's just an old abandoned building. The Mayor doesn't even exist. My father is definitely not there."

He was quiet a moment. Then he said, "People need myths. Sometimes when things are bad, we want someone to blame. Maybe that's why you had Gone."

She didn't understand. But his voice smiled at her as he said goodbye, and then there was a huge shaking, and cracking and creaking, and the Thing rose up into the air, slowly, slowly, like it was fighting gravity. It got higher and higher, until she was straining to see it, shielding her eyes from the vicious sun through her visor.

And then, suddenly, it was gone. She looked around, waiting for the world to get better. But nothing happened.

And then something did. Right on her nose.

A raindrop. And another, and another.

She walked home, through the rain, watching people come out and stare at the sky like a miracle had happened.

Somewhere in a building among many buildings, no more dangerous than any other, a bassoon started a jolly tune, and a tiger stopped pacing like a caged thing, and stared out of the window at the sky.

About Jax Goss

Jax Goss is an editor and writer. She is a wandering South African who has settled in New Zealand. She lives in Dunedin, for the moment. She is currently employed full time as the mother of a very small human, and writes and edits on the side. She expects this situation to stay the same for a while, but she has long ago learnt that nothing ever goes the way she expects.

She spends a large amount of her time gathering tales and poems and art and sending them out into the world in various forms, and thinks that this may be her vocation. She has edited a number of anthologies for Solarwyrm Press, and her stories have appeared in a variety of places. You can follow her wayward journey at her website: jaxgoss.wordpress.com.

Glass Fifty-Three

by Craig Pay

"Ashy-slut! Ashy-slut!" Zezolla's two older sisters have turned their taunts into a song as they dance around the bedroom. Anna is holding the vacuum cleaner canister above her head, covering the room in a settling layer of dust. "Your room's covered in ash!" Pru cries. They both laugh, continuing their dance.

"Stop it!" She yells at them. "Just stop it!"

The vacuum cleaner is confused, trundling around, trying to suck up all the falling dust. It keeps butting into their ankles, apologising every time it does so.

Zezolla tries standing on her tiptoes, making a grab for the canister, but she can't reach it. Her sisters are too tall. They just shove her away. Their father must have been fair-haired and tall, narrow-framed, certainly an Anglo. Her own father was obviously dark-haired and short, probably an Ethnic. This is as much as they all know. Never any names. Their mother has always refused to give them anything more.

Both fathers, however, share one similarity: a mutual absence. And this single connection seems to be enough for the sisters to hate her. Devise, each and every day, some new torment to apply.

Her sisters leave once the canister is empty. Standing there in her room, sneezing and wiping her nose, Zezolla watches the dust settle.

Her eyes are itching. She blinks.

It isn't quite ready yet, but when it is, they'll be sorry.

oooooo

Detective Bezaubern Prinz hooks a pencil into the pistol's trigger guard and lifts it up for a closer look. The gap is barely large enough for the pencil to fit through. The pistol looks something like an old world Derringer with two barrels, one over and one under, heavy calibre, at least a .44. But it's nothing like any kind of gun that he's ever seen before. He uses the pencil to turn the pistol around, watching the light bounce and refract. Glass. The pistol is made from some kind of glass.

The body is lying face down on the marble steps with an exit wound in its back the size of his clenched fist. A narrow trail of blood has dripped away down the stairs. The hole is large enough that he could easily slide his hand in without touching the sides, perhaps poke a finger through to the cool stone beneath. He decides not to do that, not after the last time.

The butler. At least he can cross that name off his list of suspects, which makes a change.

He hears the echo of a door opening and closing again somewhere beneath him, down in the entrance hall. Then the sharp clicking of footsteps, pausing for a moment, before coming up the stairs towards him.

Later, he will wonder why he did what he is about to do. He slides the pistol off the end of the pencil and into the palm of his hand. Slips the gun inside his jacket pocket.

oooooo

Zezolla ordered the pattern from a friend of a friend of someone they knew who was, in turn, a friend of someone else. And so on. The image of the old woman's face that hovered in her room was so grainy that the colour of her eyes and hair were indistinct. Zezolla couldn't even tell whether the woman was Anglo or not. Given the nature of the purchase that she made that day, this was, perhaps, the point.

She told the old woman what she wanted and the pattern arrived just a few moments later: an old world scroll bearing a plain wax seal which flew in through the window and settled on her outstretched palm. Zezolla took the scroll over to her old three-dee and stared at the faux wax seal until it broke. The scroll then vanished in a blocky burst of pixels.

Nothing for a moment. Then the print-head began to move, creeping back and forth, making a low grinding noise. After a while, she picked up the heavy machine and hid it away in the back of her wardrobe where her sisters would never find it. With the wardrobe doors shut she could barely hear it still working away.

That first day she checked every hour. The print-head carried on moving, but it didn't seem to be doing much of anything at all. The next day she checked it three times: morning, afternoon and then again later that evening. Still nothing. After a few more days she became bored and forgot all about it for a week or so. Her sisters continued their torture. Again and again she helped the vacuum cleaner clear all the dust from her room, her sisters' taunts still hanging in the air: "*Ashy-slut! Ashy-slut!*"

She went to her wardrobe. The three-dee was covered in a fine layer of dust and for a moment she wondered whether it had finally stopped working altogether. Then the print-head snapped to one side before beginning another pass. There, on the plate, she could see the faint outline of a barrel, grip and trigger.

She topped up the liquid in the print-head.

And waited.

oooooo

"Hey, Bez." A woman's voice from behind him.

He grunts in return. She always calls him that. Never his full name. She probably can't even pronounce it; none of them can.

"Messy," she says eventually, standing next to him on the stairs, looking down at the body.

He grunts again.

"No weapon?"

He makes a non-committal noise. Somehow this is easier than lying.

"Crime-scene guys here any moment," she says.

"I know," he says.

She turns to leave and hesitates. "Well, come on then. They'll need to scan the place. Get their bugs down."

They walk down the stairs together. The pistol feels huge in his pocket, knocking against his ribcage, though not as hard, he supposes, as the bullet that knocked against the butler's.

"You know you shouldn't be here," she says. "Contamination."

He shrugs. They both know that the bugs will ignore his DNA. Scan all other traces for correlation with the Citizen Register. She knows that he knows, but she still likes to make the point. Three years out of Academy to his ten and she's already his boss, because she's Anglo and he's not.

That's why they're here: an Anglo house in an Anglo suburb. If this was the city, where all the Ethnics live stacked up on top of one other, then no one would care. It's a wonder that they let an Ethnic like him out this far, beyond the city bounds. They must be short on numbers tonight.

Zezolla has to use her right hand to clean away the greasepaint and dust from her face because her hand is still hurting from the pistol. With every sweep of cotton wool her face becomes less Anglo, more Ethnic, though it will never be more than half of each no matter how hard she scrubs (and she's tried).

With the dress and the paint her sisters hadn't recognised her at the party she followed them to. Their gaze met hers, they nodded and frowned, recognising something but certainly not putting two and two together, even when she spoke to them to tell them they were wanted upstairs.

That part of the plan had worked. She'd bought the dress from the grainy-faced woman hovering in her room. The woman said that the dress would arrive the following day and it did.

Before she left for the party, she had visited the sisters' room and watched the vacuum cleaner as it rolled around. She removed the canister, held it above her head and upended it. She held her breath as the dust settled in her hair and cascaded down her face and body. Finally, she shook her head and took a breath. Sneezed. A lot.

DNA bombing. That's what the old woman called it. So when the Polizei bugs scanned the room -- the room where the two sisters would be lying with a bullet lodged in each of them -- the bugs would only see the two sisters and no one else. That was the theory.

But the butler stopped her on the stairs. Saw who she was -- *what* she was. His eyes narrowed and he called out: "Hey, you're an Ethnic! What you doing here?" He was going to start yelling.

So, she had to shoot him. Tight where it hurt: in the heart, out the spine.

But the pistol, it turned out, didn't like her. It bucked and bit and jumped from her grip. So she ran, leaving the pistol behind. Down the marble steps and out of the front door of the grand Anglo house, her plan in tatters.

Rather like the butler's cummerbund. Not to mention his ribcage.

Polymer-acrylic frame, custom .53 caseless over-and-under. One barrel empty, one still loaded. No metal. Deliberately undetectable.

Bez is standing in his single-room city apartment. He turns the pistol over in his hands. It's cold. Ice. Making sure that the safety is on, he tries to squeeze his forefinger through the trigger guard, but it won't fit. He tries each of his sausage fingers in turn. None of them will fit, not even his pinky. A woman. An Anglo woman at an Anglo party with dainty little fingers.

The phone buds in his ears begin to buzz and, after a moment, he takes the call.

A young female voice. His boss. "Hey, Bez."

He grits his teeth.

"The bugs found four traces," she says. "The butler--"

"Obviously," he says.

She hesitates for a moment before continuing. "The butler, two sisters who went to the party together, and you Bez. You should be more careful."

He sighs.

"I'll send you the address for the sisters. Meet me there." She cuts the call.

oooooo

Zezolla hears voices downstairs: her mother, her sisters and another voice, a man. She feels excitement for a moment. Her missing father, perhaps? She hopes so. Or she will need to buy another gun that will hold more bullets.

Making her way down to their musty kitchen-come-lounge-come-diner, she sees her mother and her sisters as well as a man and now another woman, a young Anglo woman. The man is certainly not the sisters' father -- he's Ethnic for starters -- in fact he's too young to be the father of any of them. He holds up a Polizei ID card. The Anglo woman shows a similar card of her own.

They start to explain why they're here. They all sit down, except Zezolla, who's ignored and left standing.

"Who's she?" The woman looks over at her standing there. "Your maid?" She makes a shooing motion with one hand. "You can go now. We need some privacy."

"Oh no!" Pru says.

"She's our sister--" Anna says.

"*Half*-sister," Pru adds, giving Anna a frown.

Anna smiles. They both titter.

The Anglo Polizeiwoman asks all the questions. The Ethnic Polizeiman keeps staring at Zezolla. She would feel uncomfortable at this attention if he didn't have such nice eyes.

The twins start to become upset. Zezolla hasn't really been paying attention but it would seem that the Anglo woman is accusing them of something. Ah yes. The butler at the house. Their

DNA all over his body. This could turn out quite well after all.

Then the Ethnic Polizeiman says, "They didn't do it." He reaches inside his jacket and brings out the pistol. The Anglo woman demands to know what's going on. He says, "I found it, right next to the body, so . . ." He shrugs. "I kept it."

The Anglo woman stares at him. "That's it Bez, final straw! You're out after this."

Bez. Such a nice name. To go with his eyes.

He passes the pistol to each of the sisters in turn, first Pru and then Anna. He asks them to hold it, to try and get a finger on the trigger. They can't, not with their big fingers. "See," he says to the Anglo woman, "they couldn't have."

Zezolla feels his eyes on her again. He hands her the pistol. She slides a finger through the loop of the guard, resting a finger on the trigger.

The Anglo woman nods. "I see.'"She stops smiling when Zezolla points the pistol in her face. The woman slides a sideways look to the Ethnic Polizeiman -- to Bez. "It's not loaded, is it?"

He shrugs. "Maybe."

She sighs. "Idiot! Well, now you're both screwed once we get out of here."

Zezolla feels a hand on her shoulder. "Come on." It's Bez. He pulls her towards the door. Outside, he bundles her into a car. Not a Polizei car, which is disappointing, just a normal car like everyone flies.

Up, away from the city, into the sky, with the countryside rolling away beneath them. They don't say anything to each other. They fly for what feels like hours. She's still holding the pistol when a yellow light begins to flash on the dash and the car drifts down to land in a field.

"We're out of gas," Bez says. "We'll have to walk."

So they walk, across one green field after another, scrambling over rough stone walls or picking their way through old razer-wire fences. They finally get around to talking. She tells him about her missing father, being treated badly by her sisters. He tells her that it's been pretty much the same for him all these years.

After a while, she can hear sirens in the distance. They head for a nearby oak tree with a great canopy which reaches right down to the ground. He suggests, "We can hide up here."

"But what about their cameras?" she asks. "Won't they just see us?"

Bez is already climbing. He helps to pull her up. They sit there on a branch next to each other.

He takes her hand -- the empty hand without the gun -- and peels back her fingers to drop some bullets into her open palm. "I

41

printed these for you."

She lets herself lean in towards him. His smell settles around her like some kind of kindred memory.

The sirens get closer.

> *Bez and Zezolla,*
> *sitting in a tree,*
> *locking and loading,*
> *their fifty-three.*

ABOUT CRAIG PAY

Craig Pay writes crossover literary/genre fiction. His short stories have been published in various magazines receiving positive reviews from the *Guardian* newspaper, *Interzone* and *Strange Horizons*. In 2011 he won the NAWG David Lodge trophy. In 2012 he completed a Master's Degree in Creative Writing at Bolton University receiving a distinction and the Vice Chancellor's Prize. Craig runs a writing group in Manchester and he enjoys Chinese martial arts. He sometimes dreams in Chinese.

Craig has recently completed a historical-fantasy novel set in 19th century Colonial China and he is now working on an SF-mythological novel set in Titan orbit during the 22nd century. You can get in touch via his website: http://craigpay.com

Tiesa's Truth

by Dominica Malcolm

"You cannot tell a lie." These were the oft repeated words in Tiesa's youth, spoken by her mother.

Though she had never thought to test her, when Tiesa was but six years of age, she questioned her mother, "Why?"

"The Goddess of Little Folk forbade it for all truth fairies like us," she said. "Should a curse fall upon one of us that allows untruths to be uttered, the green blood that gives zir life will bubble and burn from the inside out unless ze corrects zirs error within one cycle of the sun."

Curses were so uncommon in The Garden of Meilė, where they lived, that one could assume they did not exist at all, but that did not stop her mother's words from scaring Tiesa. Having the chance to utter a lie scared her more than the possibility of humans discovering their garden. It seemed far more likely, for humans were creatures of myth.

The elders in the garden took much delight in talking to youngsters like Tiesa, telling them tales of human destruction, warning them of what fate might have in store should they follow the same paths of hatred and deception.

On one occasion, Elder Kaleem---a wisdom fairy---had gathered together truth fairies of seven and eight years old to discuss the dangers of the past. They sat in the grass and looked up at their elder as he spun his words whilst sitting atop a mushroom.

"They wiped each other out," he claimed, "in what humans called the Last Great War. It was so called for all that remained at the end was perhaps five percent of those who had existed when the war began."

"What happened to the rest of them?" Tiesa asked Elder Kaleem.

"The Goddess of Purity wreaked havoc on their fertility. They died out because they could no longer reproduce. Punishment for their sins."

"That's a pile of gnome snot!" came a voice on the opposite side of Kaleem to where Tiesa was sitting.

Tiesa glanced at the dissenter. It was Audra, a girl Tiesa had generally avoided, mainly because she was popular. Tiesa feared making a fool of herself in front of her.

Audra continued, "My mother says that even though you're a wisdom fairy, doesn't make you right like us truth fairies have to be. Where's your evidence humans ever existed at all?"

"Just because your opinion is true to you, doesn't make you right, either," Tiesa spouted back. Immediately her hands covered her mouth, wishing she hadn't said anything.

Audra stood up, seething. "Oh, yeah?"

"Girls!" Elder Kaleem yelled, also standing. "That's enough."

Audra flew off in a rage, taking most of the other girls with her, and Tiesa wanted to crawl into a mole hole and die. The only girl who had not followed was Jadvyga, but Tiesa barely noticed because she was busy worrying about how much her face flushed red in response to the boys laughing.

"Perhaps you should go home, Tiesa," Elder Kaleem said. "It's going to be difficult for me to continue this lesson if you're here."

Not wanting to argue with the elder and make things worse, Tiesa nodded and left the circle. Too ashamed of herself, Tiesa felt like she didn't deserve to call herself a fairy at all. She avoided using her wings and walked home alone, back to the oak tree in which she lived.

When Tiesa arrived, she interrupted her mother picking petals that she could fashion into dresses.

"You're home early," her mother said. "What happened?"

"I got kicked out because the boys were laughing at me," Tiesa said. "Mother, why am I so different? Why doesn't anyone like me?"

"Oh, Rose Petal," her mother said, using an affectionate name for her daughter. "I think sometimes it just takes a little while to find the right friends."

Tiesa frowned. She didn't want to wait. She wanted everyone to like her right then.

Unfortunately, things didn't seem to get any better as she aged. Feeling so much like an outsider, Tiesa instead spent more time with fairies older than her, rather than ones her own age. After the laughing incident, Elder Kaleem agreed to tutor her on her own.

When she was eleven, he told her, "It is rumoured that humans still exist in coastal towns. They dare not venture inland to places like Meilė, for they fear something they call 'nuclear fallout' and 'radiation poisoning': side effects from their last war."

"How long ago did the War end, Elder?" Tiesa asked, growing ever more curious about the possibility of human life.

"It is hard to say," Kaleem told her. "The records I have seen detailed the war ending in twenty-three fifty-four AD, but I have been unable to determine what year that corresponds to in our world."

"Do you think they will ever find us?"

Kaleem shook his head. "Now I think that's enough for today."

That night, the dreams started. Images flashed in her mind, but Tiesa did not know what to make of them.

When Tiesa reached her adolescence, she watched others of her kind with confusion on her face as they partnered up and started mating rituals. Male fairies held little interest to her, but she supposed this was a ritual she, too, should follow, if she was ever going to feel included.

Assuming she was just a late bloomer, Tiesa approached Jadvyga, who had already found herself a mating partner. Though Tiesa had never actually spoken to Jadvyga before, she seemed to be the most approachable. After all, she recalled that she was the only girl from her childhood who didn't laugh at her at some point. Tiesa had also observed Jadvyga talking with other fairies with grace and compassion.

After exchanging formal introductions, Tiesa asked, "You seemed to find your mate so easily. How am I supposed to find mine?"

Jadvyga sighed. "I was betrothed," she said. "If it were not for my mother, I do not think I would have one."

It was not the promising discussion Tiesa had in mind. Not knowing what to say next, she spread her wings and flew upwards into the vines, escaping the embarrassment of trying to communicate further.

Whilst sitting on a leaf, Tiesa felt her face flush. She tried to wrack her mind with ideas of ways she could have finished the conversation, but came up with nothing. Then the memory of Jadvyga's face, hidden behind brown curls, entered her mind. Jadvyga's last words were repeated. *I do not think I would have one.* Tiesa wondered what she had meant by that. Jadvyga was very friendly, and could probably have had her pick of any male she so desired. Did it then mean she would have preferred not to have a mate?

Tiesa sighed. Flying off as she did likely meant she no longer stood a chance in finding out. Her heart felt heavy with the weight of realisation. Jadvyga may have been the only other fairy who felt like she did.

Weeks passed, and Tiesa had little contact with anyone beyond her parents. When she finally decided to venture further than a metre from her home, she walked through a small mushroom village. Sitting outside one of the mushroom houses was a gaunt gnome named Kazimeras. Tiesa had seen him around before, but they had never officially met. The only thing Tiesa knew about Kazimeras was that he was a generation older than her.

Kazimeras was smoking a reed when he noticed Tiesa and waved her over. He offered her a puff, but she declined, so he placed his right hand on his chest in greeting. Tiesa greeted him back the same way.

"It is good to see you out and about again, Tiesa," Kazimeras said, dropping his hand to his side. "Your mother seemed worried about you when she came by my stall last week."

"It is hard to want to get out and talk to others when I don't know how. The last time I tried, I didn't even say goodbye."

"Oh, you poor girl," Kazimeras said, putting out his reed. He took one of Tiesa's hands in his own, and brushed the back of it with his other one. "I used to have the same problem. Perhaps I could mentor you?"

Tiesa pulled her hand away and hesitated. She had a funny feeling about Kazimeras, but she didn't know if she was just scared, especially because she had never spoken to another gnome before. Her parents hadn't really done the best job of exposing her to other races of magical folk, even though there were instances where it was necessary to interact with them.

On the other hand, Tiesa realised she would probably not get another opportunity like this one. Then a part of her wondered if Kazimeras could be her potential mate. Was that allowed? Maybe the reason she wasn't interested in the male fairies was because they were too similar to herself.

With a smile, Tiesa placed her palms together in front of her and bowed. "I would like that very much," she said as she stood straight again.

Over the next few weeks, Tiesa and Kazimeras met regularly at his stall as he closed it up for the evening. They would walk around the pond, where Kazimeras would generally find a reed he could smoke as they talked. Tiesa felt herself growing in confidence with every day that passed where he didn't run away in fright at the things she said to him.

"I have nightmares," Tiesa confessed one day.

Kazimeras looked concerned. "What do you dream about?"

"Humans returning, and slaughtering us all with their weapons. Blades slicing off heads everywhere I look."

"My poor child," Kazimeras said. "We must remedy this, and I think I know just how."

oooooo

On the eve of the summer solstice, Kazimeras insisted that Tiesa go with him on a quest to stay up all night to watch the sunrise, and he wanted to invite two other truth fairies, Audra and Rozalija. Tiesa didn't know Kazimeras was even friends with these girls, but they were known to her as a couple of the most opinionated of her kind.

Tiesa recalled a memory from her younger years. She had been flying between lavender-coloured *Hepatica nobilis* flowers, collecting petals for her mother to fashion into dresses.

Audra had seen Tiesa from above and called, "You're not going to wear *that* colour, are you?"

Not knowing how to respond, Tiesa bit back her tears and hovered on the spot. That's when Rozalija joined Audra's side. Whilst Audra was clothed in white petals, Tiesa considered that perhaps Audra did not enjoy colour. She briefly wondered if Rozalija, who was wearing a pinkish-red, would come to her rescue. Tiesa watched them natter briefly amongst themselves while she remained frozen but for her fluttering wings.

"*Zibute!*" Rozalija said, referencing the flower's name. She laughed as she flew closer to Tiesa. "If you're going to pick petals from that ugly flower, at the very least get the blue ones."

Tiesa couldn't bear to hear another word and flew straight home to her mother.

"Why are you crying, my dear?" her mother asked as she handed the petals over.

She had been wounded, and it was too fresh for her to talk about, but her mother knew her well and she didn't have to say a thing.

"Rose Petal, don't worry about what other fairies think. You are kind, and special. Your unique view of the world makes you so much better than the judgemental of our kind."

Tiesa continued to weep, but now it was because she knew how lucky she was to have a mother like that.

They had been young then, and after a few other similar instances from Audra and Rozalija, Tiesa had learned to avoid them. Perhaps over the last few years they had grown up a bit. Wanting so much to believe it was possible, Tiesa agreed to Kazimeras's quest.

The night started out well, with Rozalija taking Tiesa's hand and apologising for the past. Tiesa smiled at her. Audra was not so forthcoming with such an acknowledgement, but her placid attitude was still better than her former judgemental one.

Kazimeras led the fairies to a circle of shiny black rocks that sat right at the edge of the pond. It seemed the perfect place to sit and talk the night away, and Tiesa was hopeful for new friendships forming. Fireflies danced in the reeds after dark, and with the clouds covering the moon, they were the only light source.

"Let's tell creepy stories," Kazimeras said. "The atmosphere is perfect, and I am the king of horror."

Whilst Tiesa was skeptical, the other two fairies were excited. Tiesa began to wonder if they had borne witness to his tales in the past. If so, why had she never been introduced to them? Weren't they good friends?

"I'll go first," Rozalija said. "Have you heard about what happened to the humans?" The question was rhetorical, and Rozalija didn't wait for an answer. "Because I heard that the ones that survived walked around looking like their faces had been ripped off by bears."

"That's stupid," Audra interrupted. "Humans are just stories, myths. No one has ever actually *seen* one."

"I have."

Everyone looked to Tiesa, so sure that she couldn't be telling the truth, despite the fact she was a truth fairy.

"Do tell," Kazimeras prompted.

"I want to hear one of your stories first." Tiesa's shyness was showing. She didn't want to risk their friendship by telling the story, and hoped that by letting Kazimeras go first, they would forget she had said anything by the end.

"Alright then," Kazimeras said. "This is a true story. There is an evil gnome, who is known to us as Marijus, though he rarely takes on that name himself. He befriends fairies, taking up to several years to gain their trust, in order to get closer to them."

A chill rose up Tiesa's back as she began to wonder if it's odd for fairies and gnomes to be friends.

"What's wrong with that?" Audra asked.

Kazimeras's lips turn up in a wicked curl. "Because," he said, "he's only going to kill them in the end."

Tiesa bit her lip, while the other two fairies gasped.

"Marijus really hates their rotting petal dresses," Kazimeras continued. "In his head, he's licking his lips, wanting to rip the flowers away and taste their flesh."

Feeling self-conscious and beginning to worry that Kazimeras was actually Marijus, Tiesa threw her arms across her body so they held the opposite side's shoulders. Audra and Rozalija leaned in closer to him in eager anticipation.

"So one day he befriends the youngest fairy he ever has. She's a cute little redhead."

Audra and Rozalija are both blonde, but Tiesa didn't miss the point. He was talking about her. She was the redhead.

"This fairy is the most annoying Marijus has ever met, but he knows that will make the meal he has of her so much more delicious when she realises how much she has been lied to."

Tiesa's eyes began to well up, but she was determined not to show her anger. She didn't even question why she was angry rather than afraid. There he was admitting he was a murderer. Or was that a lie too?

Audra blew him off. "Nah, that's stupid too." She turned to Tiesa. "Let's hear the dork's human story now."

By the time Tiesa heard the word "dork," she was furious, but she was determined not to show it. She would get her own back. She would tell a horror story so scary they would all wet themselves.

Though Tiesa had never actually seen a human in real life, they came alive in her nightmares. Being a truth fairy meant she could not lie, but that did not mean she had to say it came from a dream.

Starting slow, she said, "His face was covered with blood, smeared from battle wounds---both his own and those he had killed."

"Legend of the last human war occurred many years ago," Audra interrupted.

"Oh, the battle was not a war. This human just liked to kill."

Rozalija shuddered, but Audra remained skeptical and Kazimeras rolled his eyes.

"He was here, in the Garden of Meilė," Tiesa warned. "When everyone else was asleep."

A rustling sound was heard in a nearby bush, and it was late enough now that all the other magical creatures who lived in the garden were expected to be asleep. The fairies jumped on their stones, switching from sitting to standing. Tiesa was spurred on.

"He saw me, too," she said, "but told me I would be protected if I would give up others of my kind. He did not tell me what he would do with them, but my guess is it wasn't good."

"What did you say?" Rozalija asked, hanging on Tiesa's every word.

"Well, I'm still here, aren't I?"

Audra rolled her eyes this time. "No one's gone missing."

"Not yet," Tiesa said.

The rustling moved to a closer bush, and Rozalija clambered closer to Audra, hugging her tight.

"This isn't scary at all," Kazimeras intervened.

"Shh," Rozalija said, and prompted Tiesa to continue. "You're not going to let him take us, are you?"

"Why should I protect you?" Tiesa asked. "After all the teasing you put me through when I was younger?" She threw on her own wicked grin, and it felt more evil than the one Kazimeras had worn earlier. "I already decided to give him everyone who has done me wrong." Shooting a glare to Kazimeras, she added, "And he said I needn't only give him fairies. Gnomes would also do."

Kazimeras remained steady, until the rustling had moved to the reeds just beside him. Daring not to look around, he and the other truth fairies took off immediately. Tiesa sighed as she watched them disappear. She knew not what had been making the sound, but given her continued lack of friendship, Tiesa assumed it was probably a small animal lurking.

As Tiesa remained on her rock, she hoped whatever it was would just come out and do its worst to her. She was tired of the nightmares, and even if the other little folk had been mean, she no longer wished to scare people away.

Hoping for it to be a fox, Tiesa finally spoke to the reeds. "Come out, then. Just get it over with and eat me."

As she watched the reeds, a brunette fairy wearing a lavender *Hepatica nobilis* petal dress emerged.

"Jadvyga?" Tiesa asked. "What are you doing here?"

Jadvyga smiled, and took Tiesa's hands in her own, "I had heard Audra and Roza talking about scaring your petals off, and I didn't want to let them get away with it."

"So you helped me scare them instead?" Tiesa furrowed her brow. "But why? I thought you wouldn't have wanted to even see me again after I flew away in the middle of that conversation."

Shaking her head, Jadvyga brushed a hand down Tiesa's bare arm. "I know you were just shy, and feeling awkward. I like you, Tiesa. I want to get to know you better."

"So you want to help me find my mate?" Tiesa asked.

"Yes, but one who actually suits you," Jadvyga said, her lip turning up on the side. "I left mine because he wasn't right for me. Talking to you made me realise that was possible."

Tiesa felt ants crawling in her stomach. "So who do you think suits me?"

With a smile that made Jadvyga's eyes twinkle, she said, "Me."

About Dominica Malcolm

Dominica Malcolm is the author of *Adrift*, a speculative fiction novel about a 17th century female pirate who travels into the 21st century. Recently, she also published *Amok: An Anthology of Asia-Pacific Speculative Fiction*, which includes 24 stories by various authors. She can be found online at her blog/web site, http://dominica.malcolm.id.au, which also links to other places you can find her. Aside from writing, Dominica is also a stand-up comedian, avid traveller, and has delved into filmmaking. Though born and raised in Australia, she spent five and a half years living in Malaysia with her husband and children, and is now based in California.

Something Wicked This Way Spun

by A.D. Sams

In a small cottage on the edge of a flowered lane, lived a shy, but lovely young woman. Her name was Lilia and she was a most gifted seamstress. People came from far across the land to commission her work. Men, women, children, and even a stuffed bunny sought out her stylish and lovely designs.

Lilia was a woman driven by her spirit. Her heart was as big as her talent which meant that she made beautiful clothes with warmth and inspiration. When Lilia was happy, her garments turned those that wore them into captivating and magnetic folk. On the rare occasion that she was sad, her clothes were a bit more moody and those that wore them became melancholy. They were something deep and beautiful together in a dance.

She put the biggest parts of her heart, though, in the clothes she made for the Duke's son, Dmitri. He always looked perfect in everything he wore and she took extra pride in tailoring his things. Truth be told, Lilia loved Dmitri, and Dmitri, who was too absorbed in himself, barely took notice. The sight of him made her heart flutter and her hands became a pin cushion when he was near. She did not care about her hands. She only cared about this man who put her heart into a whirling dervish, the handsome Dmitri in the beautiful suit.

"Lilia," he would say while admiring his reflection in the mirror, "you know exactly how to dress a man." While this was true, she knew his lines better than any other. Dmitri would leave her a small tip and walk down the lane in his brand new suit of clothes without ever looking back. Lilia would run to the window and watch him until even his shadow fell from her sight.

One day, a woman brought her daughter to see Lilia. The daughter, Inessa, had never liked Lilia, or anyone else from what Lilia had witnessed. And even though she was a most beautiful girl on the outside, on the inside Inessa was bitter and ugly. Be that as it may, Inessa was engaged, and they had come to commission a wedding dress.

As always, Lilia designed a beautiful gown. There was a classic touch to the elegance of the dress, one that would make Inessa the talk of every town within four days ride of the castle. The bride, however, felt it would be better with some modifications and forced Lilia to include her many gaudy suggestions. Gold gilded flowers where they didn't belong. A sash that covered intricate stitching. Puffed sleeves large enough to make a separate gown. The dress had turned into a terrible mess, and it was not by Lilia's doing.

On the first day of fitting, Lilia brought out the the base of the gown so Inessa could try it on before the adornments were in place. She stood in front of the mirror, gazing at her own reflection and admiring her own figure. Her mother mindlessly praised Inessa until the girl finally seemed satisfied.

"Mother, this wedding will be perfect! Now, he has asked that there be a salute during the ceremony, and I don't care how much he likes his friends, they are not going to be in my wedding. He has enough money to pay them to sit just like the rest of the guests. I thought that my plan would work much better, so I've had a salute of swords designed as part of the decoration. Since gold would look stunning with my hair, I'm having a row of swords dipped in gold that point to the sky and surround the back of the stage," she rambled. Lilia noticed the tight expression on her mother's face as she said this.

"Do you really want a row of gold skewers in your wedding, dear? What will the cost be for such a thing?"

"Oh shut up, mother! It will be gorgeous. Dmitri will pay for whatever I want. Including this dress," she said as she leered at Lilia from the corner of her eye. "Duchess Inessa," she said with a smug expression, as if she had been repeating it since the day their marriage was arranged.

When Lilia heard his name, the pin in her hand slipped and stabbed her thumb. A red dot immediately formed and threatened to roll off of her skin and onto the white fabric.

"Watch it, you troll! If you get anything on my dress you will start from scratch and we will expect the price to reflect your mistakes. Of course, I could just go elsewhere."

"No, no. I'm sorry. It didn't get on the dress," Lilia said, slipping a small bit of cloth around the wound on her hand as a bandage.

She was in no way prepared for what she heard, and to lose her Dmitri to such a horrible girl... Lilia didn't know what to do.

"You don't really think Dmitri would have ever fallen for you, do you?"

Lilia felt her heart stop and a cold shard raced through her stomach.

"Do you think people don't know about your infatuation or how you watch him through your window? Do you think Dmitri doesn't know?" Inessa laughed as a cruel grin spread across her lips. "You're a joke to him. You and your long spindly fingers. Do you know what he calls you? He calls you the Spider Woman and he never thinks of you otherwise. You are nothing and no one to him. Remember that as best you can. Now," she leaned ever so slightly towards Lilia, whose face had paled to a milky hue, "get back to work, seamstress, before I go and tell all of my wealthy friends that you ruined my wedding dress."

Lilia's heart splintered piece by piece and something inside her darkened under a shadow. She said nothing and continued working, her head down and her face burning. Her Dmitri would never say such things. He couldn't have.

Inessa and her mother finally made their way out, leaving Lilia shattered. She looked down at her hands, something she had never given a second thought to, and saw them in their long and skinny forms. She balled her fists, squeezing against the needles she was still holding and barely felt as the tips slid into her skin.

She made the dress just as it was requested. Every evening she sewed and sewed, her hands ached, her tears dropped onto every thread. The night before the wedding, she cried until the stream from her eyes ran red. Still, she cried the red into an inky black poison. Her hands and face were covered with the dark liquid. It continued to run and cover her face. Lilia saw the dress across the room and before she knew it, she'd run her blacked hands all over the fabric and buried her face onto the front of the dress. It absorbed her until she closed her eyes.

Lilia slept.

When the morning sun touched her face, she sat up with a gasp. Panic squeezed her insides.

"Please," she thought, "let last night have been a dream." As a knock at the door echoed across the room hard enough to cause her breath to catch, she finally allowed herself to look at the dress knowing she would have to explain the mess she'd made.

It was pristine.

Other than the garish style, it was perfectly crafted and exquisite. Having been through more fittings than she had the patience for, and underpaying Lilia just because she could, the bride sent her servant to pick it up before the wedding without slipping into the final product. He was waiting at the door as Lilia willed her body to move.

The entire township had been invited, at least those that the bride felt were worthy, which certainly didn't include Lilia. She didn't care. Lilia had already decided to go and view the fruits of her hours spent with needle and thread. She had made clothes for most of those in attendance, so she knew they wouldn't think her out of place if she slipped in the back.

Lilia arrived, just as she had planned, at the very last moment. She sank into the shadows and felt at home there. From here she could see Inessa's taste spattered across the decor, and then her eyes found him. Dmitri was in the front, dressed in the last suit that Lilia had made him. He was glancing at his reflection in one of the candelabras on stage. Lilia, surprising herself, felt nothing.

"Spider woman," she whispered to herself and cringed. She was sick with embarrassment. It was at that moment she almost turned to leave, but a commotion stopped her.

A scream tore through the building, and as if on cue, Inessa burst through the doors with her mother running after. The bride was screaming down the center of the room. The sudden pains of a shattered heart had been thrust upon her, like that of a thousand pins digging into her skin. It drove her to the brink of madness, over the edge, and into the abyss. She ran down the aisle, tearing at her hair, her clothes, and her face. Dmitri watched in horror as his bride began to look on the outside just as she did on the inside. Before he could react, she had started to run directly at him.

The crazed woman flung herself at Dmitri and the both of them fell, landing on a row of upturned, golden swords. Their bodies slid down to the floor and rested in a shining heap. The crowd was silent in their collective shock.

"She was right," Lilia said quietly, "Her hair does look nice with gold." She turned and walked out of the church, cold and with a heart of grey stone.

The next morning, a packaged was placed on her doorstep. The dress, the cursed dress, had been wrapped and given back to her. She stared at it from across the room with hollow eyes, seeing the blood, Inessa and Dmitri's blood together. She picked up the dress and put it on and felt her heartache once again.

She had grown used to this feeling so instead of madness, she felt a shooting pain first on her left side, then her right. Two more areas on both sides burned and split open. Her blood mingled with the dark brown stains on the dress. Seams began to tear as she sprouted spindly legs. Lilia screamed at her reflection, her eight appendages quivered.

Her body felt like fire and everything hurt until she thought she couldn't breath. Lilia's back began to harden into a protective skeleton and her face elongated enough to skew her lovely face.

As the black liquid began to run down her cheeks for the second time, she ran out of the front door, leaving it open as if she planned to come back.

About A.D Sams

A.D. Sams is definitely a writer of southern fiction, probably a writer of dark, twisty things, and maybe a writer who hasn't quite reached a sense of potential. All of that is, of course, gross speculation. Seriously. It's just tacky. Now, She's in her mid-30's living in West Georgia with an army of fur creatures and a very healthy Imagination. She keeps it in an igloo in the back yard. Her first book, *Bayou L'Abeille*, was released in November of 2012. It's currently available on Amazon in paperback and Kindle editions. She's currently working on the next edition of *Bayou L'Abeille* stories as well as other anthology projects.

Letters From The Belly Of A Whale

by Calvin Mills

Dear Brother:

Thank you for your letter inquiring about my wellbeing, and thank you for expressing your concerns about my life here in the belly of a whale.

First let me tell you that I have at last reluctantly embraced the fact that there will be no escape. You see, I would have written sooner, but I was completely focused on several consecutive escape plots. Unfortunately, each plan, not only failed to secure my freedom, but *succeeded* in adding time to my sentence and compounding my woes. However, I am led to believe that after a certain amount of time I will eventually be released (hopefully somewhere near land). I also understand now that I was not swallowed by this whale randomly but because certain charges leveled against me by the department of Fish and Wildlife. They claim that I was poaching lobster out of season, when in reality, I was only testing my new pots and intended to let all the lobster go after I figured out how well the new pots worked. I can't discuss the case in writing, other than to emphasize my innocence. You see, everything I write to you will be reviewed, and they can use my own words against me. If anyone asks about me, please tell them I'm surviving admirably well and assure them that I am innocent, but that I could really use a good lawyer, preferably one with his own submarine.

Regarding your question, "What the hell do you eat in there?" I have to say the only half decent thing I have access to is whale meat. I simply carve it from between the ribs with my fishing knife. As you have probably heard, I was out lobstering when I was "incarcerated"... in other words, swallowed by this monster. So luckily I have my knife. Sadly, like most everything you may want or need in life, whale meat comes at a great cost. The whale goes a little wild, as you can imagine, and I suspect that he intends to add time to my sentence each time I do it, so I try not to do it very often. The thing is that in my particular case I'm stuck in unit 5612, which happens to be a sperm whale. He eats mostly giant squid. I don't know, maybe it's just the time of year for squid, but I've only seen one fish in here—some kind of shark with an enormous head. I had a bit of that, but you know, with fish it's all about freshness, so that lasted only a day or two, then I was back on the squid. And as you know, shark meat is pretty low on the seafood hierarchy.

The worst thing about the squid is that by the time they get down here to the belly they're pretty well chewed up, and of course they're covered with whale spit and whale bile, not to mention the ink. I quickly carve out a piece of meat and rinse it with salt water. There is precious little fresh water here. I only get it when unit 5612 surfaces and it happens to be raining. I gather a few drops at a time from the blowhole. In the months I've been here already I've consumed very little fresh water. I assumed I would die of dehydration, but so far I have not been so rewarded: perhaps because of the high humidity in here? I guess it could be worse; some whales eat nothing but plankton. Though an orca would be an upgrade...a little salmon, a little seal liver. Maybe with good behavior I'll get a transfer to another unit.

I've saved the worst part about the squid story for last. When 5612 swallows them, they're usually still alive. I have to be careful not to let the big ones get their tentacles around my neck. As for the size of these "colossal squid", you've got to see them to believe them. It's quite a show when one is squirming all around the belly in the throes of death, bleeding and covered in ink and whale spit, slapping the walls wildly with its tentacles. It's enough to turn a person off sushi quality calamari. But you've got to eat it while it's fresh or it goes nasty on you quick. You want it as fresh as you can get it here because before long it tastes exactly like puke.

It already smells like puke here—not surprising I suppose. This is the belly of a whale after all. I won't lie. The smell takes some getting used to. If you've ever smelled a nice ripe sea lion carcass on the beach, and if you've ever accidentally taken a big whiff of a dumpster behind a seafood restaurant on a sunny day, and if you've ever smelled the putrid vomity filth of a New Orleans French Quarter gutter on a Sunday Morning, and if you can imagine all these stenches simultaneously, you might begin to imagine how horrendous this reek really is. Curiously, there's also a hint of cinnamon.

In your letter you asked about my living quarters. My "cell" is a bit hard to describe. The first thing that grabs you is the darkness. Only when he surfaces do I get a burst of light through his spout. By the time my eyes adjust, it's gone again. So what I'm about to tell you, I've gathered slowly, not all in one moment, or day, or week even.

The most unique thing is the texture. The inside of the stomach isn't perfectly smooth. It's covered with these organic shapes. It's a little like intestines or brains—you know, lots of curvy lines. But it's overall flattish. It's a little taller than my living room at home. I'm guessing ten-foot ceilings. Of course there's no furniture to speak of unless you count the dead squid I sometimes use as a pillow, or a sofa, depending on its size. I experimented with a giant squid hammock, but it proved to be almost as impractical as it was unpleasant, and eventually it succumbed to the digestive enzymes and fell apart. In regards to the floor, it's a damned lucky thing I was wearing my fishing gear when I was swallowed. I mean, I really lucked out on that account. I happened to be wearing my rubber boots. If I didn't have them, I don't know what would have happened. The stomach acid certainly would have eaten through the skin on the bottom of my feet by now. I bet the skin would go first, then the muscle. Finally I'd be walking around on the raw bones. And the sticky soft tissue I'm forced to walk around on all day, thank God I don't have to feel it with my bare feet.

Overall I guess you could say my living space is dark and grossly inadequate. There are none of the finer things, of course, no pictures on the walls, no kitchen, no television, no garage for my hobbies, but worst of all, there aren't even any necessities. There's no running water, no prison yard for fresh air and exercise. There isn't even a bathroom. When it comes to bodily functions, I do my business in the back corner of the stomach where all the squid corpses have pretty much gone to mush. When I wake up tomorrow morning, the squid mush will have disappeared, my business having disappeared with it.

Speaking of bodily functions, you're a man. I'm sure you can imagine how horrific it is here in the masculine respect. If you think masturbation is pathetic in the real world, wait until you're forced to do it while being held prisoner in the belly of whale. Dignity? If I ever had a single drop of it, I sure don't now.

I'm telling you all the gory details, brother, because I want you to know how important it is for you to stay on the straight and narrow path. Don't ever get mixed up in anything that can get you sent to a place like this. When we were kids mom always said, "If you keep misbehaving, you'll end up in the belly of a whale." I just laughed. We all did, didn't we? It seemed pretty farfetched. Now, here I am.

Please consider me living proof that straying from the path comes with a serious set of consequences. When you love fishing as much as I do, it's real tempting to wet a line out of season. I see other people doing it all the time, and they almost never get caught. All I can say is, it isn't worth the risk.

Believe me, until you've found yourself living in the belly of a whale, you don't know what a hard life is. You don't know what "lack of dignity" means. You can't yet grasp accurate concepts of boredom and despair. But you know me, I keep truckin. What else can I do?

You asked in your letter how long they intend to hold me. Boy oh boy. You know how slow the government is with paperwork. I am yet to be notified as to exactly how long I'll be here. At least I've developed a method for documenting the number of days I have been here so far. Did you know that squid have no skeletons? They have only one bone in their entire body: their beak. I have a ritual of collecting one of these hard little triangles every day. I keep them in my pockets. I've got almost a hundred so far.

Thank you for writing to me, brother. You have no idea how incredibly boring it is in the belly of a whale. Once you get past the overwhelming horror and disgust, you spend a surprising amount of energy and time just trying to stand up and keep your balance. I mean this is a regular whale. He's swimming around, hunting squid, surfacing to breathe; this guy doesn't just sit around. And there's the darkness. That's part of the reason it has taken me so long to respond to your letter. Did you know that a sperm whale can hold his breath for an hour and a half, and he averages dives of 35 minutes? With the infrequent bursts of light from the spout, it took me three beaks to read your one page letter. It has taken me more than forty beaks to write you back.

Speaking of letters, the whale is responsible (according the International Sea Mammal Cavity Incarceration Division's official pamphlet, which I found stuffed in the stomach of a decomposing squid thirty-three beaks ago) to provide me with paper and envelopes. There are no writing implements allowed. I use squid ink, scratching it onto the paper with the tip of my fishing knife. For some unknown and bureaucratically backward reason, the whale is NOT responsible for postage. So if you want to hear from me again, please enclose a stamp or two with your next letter.

I should probably close this letter now. From the way unit

5612 is thrusting around, I'm guessing another giant squid is about to shoot through his esophagus. I've got to be ready to cut off a slab for dinner, clean it up, collect today's beak, and make sure the damn squid doesn't strangle me.

Love, your brother,
Tom

Calvin Mills is a writer of short stories, essays, and plays. His work has appeared in *Short Story, Weird Tales, The Caribbean Writer, Tales from the South*, and many other publications. He has received the Charlotte and Isidor Paiewonsky Prize, the Cooper Honors Award for Fiction, the Advisor's Prize for Fiction from Toyon, a Meritorious Achievement Award in Playwriting from the Kennedy Center ACTF for *Freak Like Me: The Musical*, and a nomination for a Pushcart Prize. He teaches at Peninsula College in Port Angeles, Washington, where he is the faculty advisor for *Tidepools Magazine* and a member of the Foothills Writers Series committee. Mills grew up behind the Redwood Curtain in Eureka, California, and lived for a decade in Little Rock, Arkansas.

The Rawheads And The Little Girl

by Danielle Forrest

The sun had set, which meant no lights. No lamps, no fires. Couldn't have the Rawheads thinking anyone lived here. Good way to get dead. Grandma was grumbling in the corner while Mom washed dishes in the sink with rain water. Dad was making sure everything was secure for the night. Deadbolts on each door, nails through the frame of each window, guns at each entry.

As I sat on the couch, which had been repaired more times than I could count, I ran my fingers over coarse stitching from a tear. I was keeping my eye out for a salvage in the old abandoned buildings. That was what I contributed to the family — I scoured the Lost Places, looking for things we could use. It was a dangerous job, but safer on a child. Easier to hide, easier to slip through small cracks. Easier to avoid the Magpies and Rawheads.

Magpies liked their shiny things and, when I saw them, I never thought too hard about whatever meat they happened to be gnawing on. Could be rabbit. Could be little girl. Magpies weren't too picky. The Rawheads, on the other hand, preferred Breeders. I was thankfully too young.

"Grandma? Tell me about the End Times?" I asked hesitantly. Grandma was the only one old enough to really remember. My parents had been kids. They didn't remember when things worked, when you could go outside without a weapon.

"Hmph," she waved my question off. "You don't need to be hearing that garbage. Just reminiscing of a world long gone. Don't do ya' no good, dreaming of the past."

Grandma continued to grumble, complaining about people as she always did. Grandma was an equalist — she hated everyone equally. A lot of the old timers were like that. So many groups were responsible for what happened, and everyone placed the blame somewhere else. The Democrats blamed the Republicans. The Republicans blamed the Democrats. The NRA blamed both. It just went on and on. If there was a group, they blamed the end of the world on another, back in the day. So, most people that remembered blamed everybody equally. After all, what was the point in placing blame? Wouldn't bring the world back.

Now? People just blamed everything on the Rawheads and Magpies. They were the modern boogeymen. Nobody knew what the Rawheads really were. They had gone by many names. Its members were called monsters, cannibals, murderers, thieves. Nobody knew the truth. It didn't keep people from making theories, though. And I suspected a lot got blamed on the Rawheads that was just individuals looking out for number one. A lot of people pass through. Not a lot of people these days have any respect for property... or life.

Magpies were a different story, though. They were most certainly real. I'd seen them. They were why no house had anything shiny on it. Magpies liked shiny things. They scavenged the Lost Places like I did. They were crazy, attacking anything that moved. Nobody knew what drove those women to madness. If they were women at all. I had no interest in finding out. All I cared about was avoiding them.

"You want a story? I'll give you a story. One'll do you some good too." Grandma started waving her finger in my direction again. The digit was so knobby, crooked, and skinny, I thought it looked skeletal. I thought it might fall off. An image popped in my head of her flinging that finger at me, the distal parts flying at my face and smacking me in the forehead before falling to my lap.

Finally, she sighed and leaned back in her chair. She looked a lot older than her years. "This is a true story. Happened a *long*, long time ago in a small town just starting to make headway. They were in the south, I believe." She shook her head. "Nasty business, that."

The South. The South was no-man's-land, a Forbidden Place. It happened before I was born. People didn't speak of the South. Smiles fell when it was mentioned. It was a good way to get smacked, mentioning the South. I never asked. I didn't want to know. Anything that could make the hardened hearts of modern Jersey-folk falter wasn't any topic I wanted to know about.

"Some say the Rawheads are men gone mad. Others say they're experiments gone wrong. Still others, they say they're the monsters of ancient folklore. Grimm's tales and the like."

Grimm's. Grandma gave me an old, battered copy of Grimm's fairytales as soon as I could read. I remember having nightmares when she'd read some of the stories at bedtime. It wasn't any sort of story a toddler should hear, let alone an infant.

Still, Grandma always said, "They'll do ya' good. Prepare you for the real world. They're monsters out there. Don't know that they got fangs, but they're vicious enough."

I knew every story almost by heart.

Like one Grandma was always lilting. Not a Grimm's, but she would always say it was good learning — because it was about the Rawheads. I think it was some real old poem, long before the End Times.

Rawhead and Bloody Bones
Steals naughty girls from their homes,
Takes them to his dirty den,
And they are never seen again."

"Anyway, one day a man came to the small town. He seemed clean enough, wholesome folk. He came, traded for what he needed, and went his way. Nobody thought any more of it.

"But then a girl went missing. Few years older than you. Sweet girl. Everbody loved her." Grandma shrugged. "Everbody ignored it, said she ran off with the man who went through town. Her parents were distraught.

"But another girl went missing, and then everyone paid attention. One girl was an anomaly, two a pattern. Girls kept on disappearing, but only girls in their teens or older. No children.

"There was one girl, a brave girl. She was in her late teens, probably. All around her, the adults were in a panic, searching and finding none of her friends. She took matters into her own hands. She loaded up her bike with weapons and supplies, and went out searching. Nobody knew the area like she did. She was a scavenger, like you. She knew every Lost Place, be it building, cave, or clearing. She knew every place a person could be hid..."

oooooo

There was a dark forest outside town. She knew it held a few caves and many clearings and meadows — a perfect place to hide. She rode out to the dark forest, and dismounted her bike. Her supplies went on her back, gun in hand. She entered the dark forest.

The ground was blackened from the End Times. The trees were black and heavy with scorch marks. Nothing had grown there in some time, yet no sun leaked through. The canopy was far overhead, not a single branch within reach. But the girl wasn't afraid. The dark forest, though scary to most, was a second home to her.

She advanced.

She made her way quickly and surely through the forest, her feet light and silent. Ten minutes turned into a half hour. A half hour turned into an hour. Still she found no signs, no tracks.

Though light was scarce in the dark forest, she could still track the progress of day. She would have to turn back soon. No point chasing ghosts at night. It was dark in daylight. It was pitch black at night. She'd just as likely get lost as find the lost.

She was just about to turn back when she saw light in the distance. A fire, from the quality and color. She inched closer, being more and more careful as she advanced on the camp. She smiled. This far out, it *had* to be someone up to no good.

A few more minutes, and she was on the edge of the camp. The camp consisted of several tents circled around a bonfire. Raucous male laughter sent a chill down her spine. The laughter, sharp and braying, muffled the sounds of whimpering and crying. She heard a female voice begging, probably from one of the tents. Then a scream.

"Oh, God," she said, covering her mouth with both hands as she turned and crouched against a tree.

"Hello, gorgeous," a rough male voice said before grabbing her by her hair.

Her head screamed in fierce pain as he dragged her across the clearing to one of the tents. She didn't remember him taking her weapons, but she no longer had them. Not that she could think to use them. All she could do was grab at the hand that held her, trying to pry his grip free, trying to lessen the pain that made it feel like her scalp was being torn off.

Echoes of male laughter trickled past the pain, registering vaguely. Everything registered as if through a fog. He let go and she fell on her face, her arms useless above her head. She groaned as her scalp continued to throb from the abuse. After a few moments of blessed silence, she got her arms under her and pushed her way to sitting. She looked up into the eyes of a man with a sinister grin on his face.

"Rawheads," she whispered under her breath, taking in the visage before her. He seemed wild, his eyes speaking of an evil that lurked in every human heart, but was rarely released. Madness lived behind those eyes. If that visage had ever been truly human, it wasn't now.

The grin only got worse as he spoke, "She'll be perfect." A gravelly voice that sent chills down her spine escaped him. But it wasn't the way his voice sounded like he'd recently tried to chug gasoline that gave her chills. It was a tone in his voice that told her the things he was capable of. It told her she didn't even want to imagine what he could, and would, do to her.

oooooo

Hours later, the camp had quieted. She lay there in the tent, afraid to move, afraid she'd wake her abuser beside her. The abrasive laughter of his comrades had dimmed hours before, with only the pitiful sounds of the tormented women breaking the silence. Beyond the pain, she only had one thing on her mind. Escape.

Slow to move, afraid to even breathe, she shifted, inching onto her hands and knees. Their leader lay asleep, deceptively boyish, innocent, in his slumber. How cruel that God would lend such an innocent exterior to such a brutal interior, even if only in sleep. In slow increments, she came to her feet, still crouching, as she moved to the mouth of the tent, listening for sounds of others. But only whimpers, and the crashing of a log on the fire as it burned greeted her ears.

She reached for the tent entrance, her hands barely shifting the coarse material enough to get an eye on the campgrounds. The fire had burned down to red embers, barely lighting the few feet surrounding it. The other tents couldn't even be seen in the darkness. She looked up toward heaven. *Please, let no one see me, God.* Then, she slipped out of the tent, aware of every stone, every stick, every bruise, cut, and possibly even broken bone. Everything hurt, but she shoved it to the back of her mind, demanding that her body push forward, ignoring the pain.

As she crept farther and farther from the fire, her heart pounded harder and harder in her chest. Dizziness started in as she pushed herself, step after step, inch after inch, not letting herself breathe deeply like she would like. Afraid the sound of one good, deep breath would give her away. Afraid they would take her back to that monster to be used all over again. A full body shiver stopped her, vibrating through her from head to heels, reminding her of her aches as she moved parts she shouldn't.

She kept moving forward, blind in the darkness of the forest. Her hands shook as she reached out in front of her, testing for obstacles. Her legs quaked with each step as she tested the ground with her toes for branches, rocks, and leaves — anything that would make a sound. Her progress seemed slow. Her journey seemed endless. Her destination seemed impossible. *They'll find me.* She had a fleeting thought they'd kill her if they caught her, but realized she wasn't so lucky. Her whole body quaked again as she tried to banish images of what they'd already done. *Just keep going. One foot in front of the other. It's not as far as you think.*

After what felt like a half hour, an hour, two, her fingers brushed against the rough bark of a tree, and she let out a soundless sigh of relief, her body sagging. But her relief was only momentary. She wasn't out of the woods yet. Literally. She could still be heard. She still had to be silent, cautious. Fortunately, these trees were dead. Leaves were rare. As she felt her way along, her heart still pounding, her breaths still shallow, her mind pulled phantom enemies out of the dark. Every little sound was a man in pursuit, gaining on her, reaching out to grab her. Every branch brushing against her was someone about to drag her back.

The darkness receded by shades. She started to make out the outlines of trees before her, just a darker shade of dark against the background. Her hands dropped to her sides, and she started scanning her surroundings. Trees as far as she could see. No movement, no other shapes. It was lightest in front of her.

She continued on, less concerned about noise. She knew she was far from the camp now. She sped up, wincing as branches cut into her feet, but not caring. It was no worse than the other pains. Without even realizing, her heart was now pounding out of exertion instead of fear. She smiled, not caring as it hurt her face, hurt the bruises, hurt the cuts. She pushed herself harder.

She was flying now. Effortless. Everything hurt, but she didn't care. She was free. She'd escaped, even her mind flitting away from what had happened, unwilling to think on it. The forest continued to lighten, and now she could see an end — a meadow up ahead. Hopefully, the same place she'd left her bike.

She erupted into the meadow and laughed, collapsing on the grass and rolling in it. She let her heart calm, taking deep breaths, letting them calm as well. After a few moments, she could almost forget what she'd been through... except for the pain. She sat up and examined herself. A couple fingers wouldn't move — probably broken. Almost every exposed inch of skin had a freshly developing bruise on it. *That's gonna be bad. The bad ones always show up that fast.* A few cuts, but not too many. Most of the cuts were on the soles of her feet, from running. Her clothes were torn to shreds and bloodied. Her shoes were gone. Her mind continued to shy away from the other abuses.

The girl looked around, hoping to see her bike. Another painful, half-hysterical laugh escaped her as she saw the bike not fifty yards away. *God always looks out for you at the strangest times, huh?* She stood and started walking, immediately regretting the little romp in the grass. Now that adrenaline wasn't flooding her system, every hurt seemed amplified. She could barely walk for the pain in her feet, but she kept on.

She reached her bike and caressed it, a tiny smile all she could manage now. *Morphine. I could really use morphine right about now.* Too bad there wasn't morphine anymore. It had specific storage requirements. No way something like that could last a Southern summer without A/C.

She mounted the bike, wincing at how the seat felt between her legs, and pedaled home in a daze, her head lolling on her neck. She shook her head every few minutes to keep herself awake. Adrenaline crash.

As she neared the town, she saw smoke in the distance. A lot of smoke. Her mind was too foggy to fabricate a meaning. She pedaled on, the dark forms of the town coming closer, becoming more defined. She blinked, a part of her psyche screaming that something was wrong but everything else too dense to catch on.

Oh no. Her jaw dropped a little, and adrenaline surged through her system once more. She pedaled harder, not even feeling the abuse on her feet, or anywhere else. *Something must be on fire.* Fire could be devastating nowadays. Not as bad as it once was, but much worse than the End Times.

At that speed, she reached the town in minutes, leaping off the bike before she'd even registered what she saw. No, *something* wasn't on fire. *Everything* was on fire. The bike slipped from her hands, clattering to the ground as shock set in.

Some of the buildings had already burnt to the ground, their blackened skeletons reaching to the sky, leaning on each other for support. Others were still in flames. *Where is everyone? Nobody's trying to put it out.*

Then she saw them. Almost indistinguishable from the burned-out buildings in the dim morning light. A blackened body, large enough to be a man. She walked forward, not even realizing it. Another man in another burned building. A boy in an alley — shot, blood staining his shirt in a crimson circle. A little girl in front of the grocer — she couldn't tell the injury, but the girl had bled out onto the sidewalk. The blood had pooled around her, absorbing into her thin, cotton t-shirt. As she walked, more bodies. Everywhere. Men. Children. No women, though. And no survivors.

Finally seeing, really seeing, she collapsed to her knees and screamed.

oooooo

"Mother? Hope? It's getting dark. Lights out," Mom whispered from over my shoulder. It was too late in the day to risk speaking above a whisper.

I nodded, and looked outside. The sun was low over the horizon, deep colors kissing the sky. It was already dark enough that a bright light might be seen. I shivered, the red color of the sky reminding me of the blood from Grandma's story. The shadows that started to stretch across the land had my active imagination dreaming up skulking monsters sneaking closer. Would they find me?

I grabbed the old oil lantern, and turned it down to its lowest setting, heading off to my bedroom. I laid it on the rough, wooden table by the bed — something my father had made — and slipped between the sheets, serenaded by creaking springs and the pounding of my own heart.

Finally ready for bed, I blew out the lantern to a blood curdling cry.

About Danielle Forrest

Danielle Forrest is an author based out of Raleigh, NC. She has been writing since elementary school after her aunt gave her a little flowered journal. Back then, she wrote short *Goosebumps*-like stories that were appropriate considering her age. She's been perfecting her novel-writing skills since middle school, when she started her first novel, *They're Here*, which is likely a pitiful excuse for literary content and one of the only books she ever wrote involving aliens. She finished her first novel, *Forever After,* sometime around 2005 and has been editing it on and off (mostly off) since then. Like most authors, life gets in the way, but she's determined to finish, and an end is finally in sight.

Her favorite writing topics include paranormal, fantasy, and science fiction. She has books about vampires, werewolves, faeries, mermaids, people with special powers, people that come back from the dead (and, no, they are not zombies), zombies (but, of course...), and nanotechnology, amongst other things. She loves books that incorporate the real world so the events of the novel could be happening right under your very nose and you'd never know.

You can read more about her here: theeternalscribe.com

The Pollen Camp

by Jan Stinchcomb

While it is still dark, my sister steals into the Pollen Camp to bring me a corset. "Our parents wanted you to have this. In case you are chosen."

I want to keep sleeping. My eyes are so heavy with pollen dust that at first I can barely appreciate Sera's offering. I focus instead on her eyes, which are dark and beautiful, flecked with gold. I don't know why I am considered the pretty one. It should have been Sera who was sent to live and work in the Pollen Camp, Sera, who lives to catch a nobleman's eye.

"They say the count is very handsome," Sera whispers before rushing away. Soon we are all awake, slipping into our clothes and gathering our baskets, getting ready to head out to the fields. The other girls begin their daily ritual of gossiping about life in the palace. They tell tales of women they have never seen: the imperious Séverine, the favored Marianne, and especially Aimée, who came from our own little village.

Aimée's success makes each of us think we have a chance. But all we do from sunrise to sunset is harvest the yellow flowers whose pollen is our sustenance and our livelihood. We make everything from pollen: soothing teas, sweet delicacies, beauty treatments, sleeping draughts. We pick flower after flower. We bend at the waist and pull. We gather and wait.

I was born for the harvest. This golden dust is my life.

When I slip on the corset, one of the other girls challenges me: "Who is that for? Do you really think you will be chosen?"

Still, she helps me, lacing me up so tight that I can barely breathe.

oooooo

Sometimes Sera and I would speak too freely about the people of the palace. The jaundiced aristocracy, we called them. The count and his ladies. A countess who could never have a child. All of them insane, crazy with their addiction--

"Fondness," my mother always corrected me. "They have a fondness for pollen. A craving. An appreciation. These are people of very refined tastes. If you work hard, you may someday have your chance in the palace. It can happen for a farm girl. Besides, you're the prettiest girl for miles, and that's all that really matters in a world ruled by one man's pleasure."

"Try to make the most of your time at the camp," Sera advised me as I prepared to leave home. I noticed how much pollen came away on her moist lips when she kissed me farewell.

We were covered in pollen. It stuck to our skin and hair, our clothing, our furniture. It coated all the buildings in yellow dust. It rose in golden clouds when my mother tried to sweep the floors. It made a lacy pattern over my best white dress.

It was in our beds and in all that we ate. In fact, I had long stopped enjoying food because of it. It made me reluctant to take anything into my body.

"Oh, you'll change your mind about that," Sera would say, giggling next to me in bed. She had a gift for finding other things to do with her time but I was driven by pollen alone.

"They say the ladies of the court wear dresses of spun gold. They say that you will make us rich if you succeed," my mother told me.

I was too frightened to inquire into the nature of this success.

"You will see a different world," said my father, somewhat wearily, as he gave me his blessing.

But the world of the camp was exactly the same as my old one, only harder.

oooooo

The most difficult time is the evening. And it is not that my bones ache or that I am homesick, although both these things are true. It is that this break from our work brings out the worst in the other girls.

There are arguments about beauty, about worthiness, about desire, until words escalate into violence that is in turn quieted by the sentries, who appear without warning to menace us with their whips. They are the only contact we have with the world outside the camp.

Our parents have forgotten us.

The palace seems oblivious.

We eat a weak pollen soup that one of the girls has thrown together. It is tasteless but calming.

I am too weak to cry. When I close my eyes, my dreams are filled with scenes of life in the palace. The faces of the noble ladies shine with a glittering powder; they wear amber and gold. Yellow roses are embroidered over endless rolls of fine fabric. Paintings of marigolds, sunflowers and daffodils hang on the walls. Canaries fly freely from room to room, finally escaping into the frigid night air.

One of the canaries comes crashing into my ribcage. I wake to find a sentry kicking me. I barely have time to grab my basket before he sets me on his horse and spirits me away to my destiny.

oooooo

When I show the palace ladies the little jar of golden jelly I have brought with me, they leap at my offering as if they are starving.

Aimée is not the girl I remember. She never leaves her tea table, where she sits with her head bowed over her preferred substance, the drink we call dirty yellow tea. She has fallen in love with the tea. When she raises her head to smile at me, I can tell that she does not remember who I am.

She was not able to produce an heir.

Neither was Marianne, but she is the favorite.

Séverine tells me that the count does not like pollen on his women and so begins my cleansing. Under the countess's supervision the other ladies advance and remove my clothing. They boil my dress in a vat of hot water, then save the water in jars, to be consumed later. They hold me under the scalding water of the bathtub as they scrub my skin and scalp and dig the pollen out from under all my nails.

(I see Aimée leave her table, strip and sink into my bath water. What's left of her body is yellow parchment stretched over tiny, birdlike bones.)

They dye my hair, all of it, the same unwholesome blond as theirs.

I am dressed in a gown embroidered by the countess herself. It is covered in yellow roses--my sister says these are a symbol of infidelity. I do not know whether this is a dare or a blessing.

I am ready for the count.

oooooo

There are no doors in the ladies' wing, not even in the chamber of the countess herself, because all the bodies here belong to the count. Someone comes in the dark of night and carries me to the countess's bed.

I wait.

As the hours pass, I begin to grow hungry. I miss my mother's dust-covered meals. I long for a cup of dirty yellow tea. I want to sleep alongside my sister and breathe in the smell of our pollen-filled house.

My head aches. It is very cold in the palace at night.

The next morning I am treated like a queen. The countess rubs my feet and forehead with a honey-colored oil. I am fed butter and marmalade, lemon tea, almond pastries dripping in honey, egg yolks. Caramel. All the ladies ask after my health. They try to anticipate my cravings. They insist that I stay in bed.

It is important to note that I never see the count.

The days pass, becoming ice cold, despite the sun, a distant yellow knot among the clouds, a stranger to us. I knew that the cold is essential for the flowers we harvest: without a winter freeze, they would never bloom. I know that last season's beauties are now bent over, heavy on their stalks, dried by the wind, waiting to be turned into meal. I know because I have gathered them in all kinds of weather.

At the camp the other girls will be working by day and weeping by night. Their hands will be covered in sores. Their hearts will break.

Down at the farm, inside my parents' house, the dust is settling, finally. The air is in its purest state, before the assault of spring.

oooooo

One morning I open my eyes to find a yellow canopy above me. I sit up. It is true: a prison of yellow roses has grown around me.

A lady's hand pierces through the rose tangle and offers me a plate. It is my breakfast. I see that the hand, which belongs to Séverine, is bloody from the thorns--an audacity of red which I know she will do her utmost to erase. I look down to see what she has brought me: sweet rolls, made of pollen flour, coated in sticky pollen glaze. My favorite, if that is possible in a world where there is only one flavor.

And so I eat. I try to stand up, but it is impossible. The smell of roses is overwhelming. My world has become a cave infused with a dull yellow light. When I think of escape, the memory of Sévérine's bloody hand comes back to me.

Later I am roused by a sword that comes piercing through the rose thicket. At first I think that this must be the count, and I am willing to accept his violence in exchange for some measure of liberty. Perhaps he will allow me to emerge from my realm of thorns, a tiny palace with its own impossible etiquette.

But it is the countess who stands before me, a sword in one hand, and something else in the other, something so small I have to lean forward to see it. But in my heart I know right away what it is. How could I not? I grew up on a little golden farm. I understood all my life that we were working in the name of reproduction. The pollen is not the actual seed, my father explained to me, it is the conveyance. The protector.

The people of the palace possess something even more valuable: the source.

What the countess holds in her hand is a lovely specimen, the stamen of some brave flower, covered in the sticky grains that are everything.

Ambitious, desperate, I reach for it.

oooooo

I clutch the stamen after the countess withdraws. Immediately the roses grow back over the space she cleared; it is impossible to tell that a sword has ever pierced my little realm. I am left alone again, despondent.

When I sleep, my dreams are filled with the girls from the camp, all of them clutching their baskets. Sera is there, too, in the untruthful way of dreams. They are all crying and wringing their hands. I feel guilty for being chosen, but when I draw near, I see that they are crying for me. They are sorry.

My corset begins to tighten until I cannot breathe. I hold out my arms, gasping for breath, begging the others to save me. But even my sister will not advance to help me.

When I wake, I realize that I am still wearing the dress embroidered with yellow roses. I remember that my corset was taken from me when I arrived. I can breathe.

And I am still holding the stamen.

oooooo

My rose chamber turns into a glowing yellow lair, which means it is the next day.

The countess again slices her way in and appears before me

with a question: "Do you know why you are here?"

I know there is only one right answer. I say merely, "Yes."

It would be unbecoming to say more. Harvesters' daughters know better than to open their mouths from the moment they step across the chilly stones of the palace floor. The countess seems pleased and even gives me a slight bow when I put the stamen to my lips. As she retreats, the roses begin filling in the space she made.

I do not know what to do with the castrated portion of flower I have taken, perhaps stolen, from the countess. I lied to her. The truth is, I do not have any answers. The truth is, I never asked my sister enough questions about the outside world. But I do know that Aimée, when it was her turn, must have swallowed the stamen. That was the beginning of her addiction: she consumed the source itself, all at once. And it did not give her a child.

The temptation to swallow the stamen is enormous. It is worshipped by the harvesters; I have never been allowed to handle one. I twirl it in my fingers. I sniff it. I consider it.

And then I make it disappear inside of me.

oooooo

The pastries begin appearing three times a day, each confection more ingenious than the one that preceded it. But each sweet meal makes me sick. I have a craving for something else, something I cannot name because I have never tasted it before.

My strength disappears. I turn soft. I discover, as I lick my fingertips, that I am growing sweeter. Glittering, golden powder begins to rub off on my pillow. The rose womb encroaches upon me, ever nearer, threatening me with its thorns.

Some small part of my old self remains. I want to leave the cold air of the palace and go back to the dust of my childhood. I want to work, but I am so weak that I can barely sit up.

When the next plate of pastry appears in the rose tangle, I grab onto the hand that delivers it. It is Séverine's. I do not let go. With the last of my strength I pull her inside the rose chamber with me.

"What will happen to me? Am I to be sacrificed? Forgotten?" I ask as we sit, bloodied, staring at each other.

Séverine does not blink. "That is all any woman can expect."

"You must help me!"

"There is no help for you. If you reject the count's seed, you will become like Aimée. There is no room for another Aimée here."

Sévérine tries to withdraw, but I stop her. "But where is the count? Why have I had no audience with him?"

Sévérine smiles the stone-wall smile of the aristocracy.

"What is your secret?" I ask her. "How are you still alive? How did you escape Aimée's fate?"

She lowers her eyes. "Perhaps I have not escaped it. Perhaps I have merely managed to maintain a balance." And then she takes my entire breakfast in her mouth and swallows it whole. I see how her skin glows afterward. She gives me a different kind of smile. It makes us equals.

I have to find the count.

I push Sévérine aside and crawl out of my fragrant prison. The thorns catch on my dress, shredding the roses that the countess embroidered. It hurts to step across the icy palace floors, but with each step, I grow a bit stronger, save for a lingering pain at my core. Something is stirring inside of me, but I know that it is not a baby.

I pass Aimée, who is bent over her tea table, stirring an empty cup. She looks up at me with an ashen face and gives me the same vague smile she offers every girl who comes to the palace. I find Marianne, the elusive favorite, sitting and embroidering in a dark corner. A little arc of light flashes with each sweep of her golden needle. When I get close to her, I realize that she is covering another dress in yellow roses. A new dress. I want to ask her who it is for.

"If you wish to speak to the countess, you must understand that she cannot be disturbed," Marianne says without looking up at me.

I ignore her, pressing on, before coming to a complete halt. Where does a harvester go after sleeping in a royal bed?

I remember my past and begin heading for the fields where I grew up.

On my way down from the palace, I have to cross the Pollen Camp.

oooooo

Outside the world is white. Snow covers everything, and I am wearing nothing but my torn dress. I fly past the sentries who stand as still as statues. I bump into one, and he falls over, weightless, nothing more than bones beneath his armor. I push another and another and get barely a grunt from any of them. They are all as desiccated as the flowers in the fields, slowly turning to dust.

The camp is empty, save for my sister, who is pale and

exhausted.

"Where are all the others?" I ask her.

But she does not answer. Instead she asks, "How is the count's health? Did you succeed?"

I realize that Sera is studying my belly. She wants me to make her rich. She herself is starving. "There is no count," I tell her.

Sera falls to her knees. The truth settles over her face like a death mask.

oooooo

I find the countess in the fields near my home. She wears the dress of a farm girl, a homespun dress the shade of wheat, but I recognize her regal features. She is not surprised to see me.

"You will be cold in that dress. And you have no shoes," she says.

The countess is gathering all the dead flowers and placing them in a crude little basket. It is the lowliest kind of work, performed in the bitter cold, usually reserved as a punishment.

She is right, I am cold, but my head is clearing. In the distance I see my parents emerge from our house and squint at me. I think I can see my sister's ghostly face staring at me from the window of the bedroom we always shared.

I know that my poor parents are hoping to see a fat belly rising out of my skirts.

"What happens now?" I ask the countess.

"It is best if you freeze first. After you die, I will bury you. But something will grow. It always does, when the golden sun returns. Then there will be another harvest."

"And if I return to the palace?" I ask, calculating my chances, knowing that she will not answer.

"You have done very well," she tells me. "But you are like all the others. There have been so many of you. There will be more."

I understand now what we should have done with the fires we built at the Pollen Camp, the fires we used for cooking, or for the comfort of warmth. A simple fire could obliterate all of this, from the stickiest stamen to the dustiest residue. I could burn these fields, kill all the seeds, set the dampness smoking, then move on to the hill, and after that to the camp. I could climb to the palace and torch all the ladies. I could free my people, what's left of us.

The countess stands and stares into my face, as she has with every mistress since the first harvest. We are each determined to destroy the other.

I don't have any fire. I don't have a sword or a whip. I have only my hands. I look at the countess's hands, which are white and weak, and then I look at mine, the strong hands of a harvester. I understand, finally, what they can do.

About Jan Stinchcomb

Jan Stinchcomb's work has appeared in *Rose Red Review*, *Luna Station Quarterly*, *darker*, *The Red Penny Papers*, *the other room*, and *PANK online*, among other places. Her novella, *Find the Girl*, is forthcoming from Main Street Rag Press in 2014. A recent transplant from Austin, she lives in Santa Monica with her husband and daughters. Visit her at www.janstinchcomb.com.

Thirst

by Andrew Patch

Astrid examined the plastic sheet as the slight breeze that wrapped around the mouth of the cave forced it to protest within its wooden frame. Though Astrid doubted it would work she had to do something before she left, give the rest of the gang something to focus upon. She looked east to see the morning sunshine cresting the ridge of the valley. Fingers crossed, later today beads of condensation would begin to form on the plastic. Once more she realigned the bucket and various tin cans she had laid out underneath doubting that any would be full later that day.

She was sick of this. It had been over three months of journeying, fourteen weeks of thirst, hunger and hardship. Following the tantalising rumour that the old trader had shared with them that night they had bartered for water. Over the orange glow of the campfire he had told them of this settlement he had heard of, where water flowed and fruit grew. They had laughed at him, dismissing him as just another madman in the wasteland. Irritated he had pulled a yellowed piece of paper out of his jacket pocket; a roughly scribbled map was upon it, he claimed that the map showed the route south to the place he called The Citadel. That had quietened their cynicism, yet the trader wouldn't agree to barter anything for the map, and it was quickly concealed back in his pocket.

Astrid suspected it was just a story to tell around the fire, something to make the old man feel important to this disparate group of kids that had banded together through circumstance and coincidence. However, that night Max became obsessed with finding the place, talking into the early hours, persuading the nine of them that they had to find this settlement. The very next day they headed south, full of wild anticipation of splashing in fountains that spurted jets of water high in the air, and drinking cold fresh water till they felt they would burst.

Now there were just six of them left. Their quest ground to a halt in this dank cave system that had been home for the past two weeks. When they had first discovered the caves it seemed they had found a potential sanctuary. A place to rest, to hide from the wasteland gangs who had killed first Django then Little Pete. Mother's scans had even detected a potential source of water, deep within the twisting maze of the cave system. So they explored, their lit torches weakly pushing back the darkness.

The AI's scans proved to be true, for they found water; sadly it wasn't a fresh underground stream rather a sad shallow pool of muddy liquid. Their disappointment was compounded, when Ruan tripped on the way back, breaking his ankle.

Ruan, ruin, ruined.

Everything was ruined.

Astrid ran her dry tongue over cracked lips, desperate for a drink, but reluctant to start on her ration of dirty water this early in the day. She pulled a smooth black pebble out from the pocket of her jeans and popped it in her mouth. She had found that the illusion of the pebble quelling her thirst had long stopped working, but still she couldn't quite give up the habit.

She picked StepMom up off the dusty floor from beside her backpack and strapped the small green box, its perspex screen scratched and marked with age, to the top of her left arm. Testing to make sure the AI was secure, she hit the [on] button. The AI squealed into life, the screen flickering yellow. Before the AI could start talking, as Steps was inclined to do, Astrid hit the [mute] button. Then she grabbed her backpack, checking her provisions for the hike a final time. It wasn't much, a small bottle of brown cave water and a few tins, whose lack of labels meant their contents were a mystery, but it was all they had spare. She double-checked that the In-Viz cloak was also within the backpack. Astrid had insisted that Max take it on his expedition, but he had refused, citing the cloak would be unable to conceal both himself and O. She was thankful that he had left it behind now.

She shouldered her backpack and stood looking down into the valley. She would follow the creek, which flowed no longer with water, but dry stone and baked earth, southwards. Following Max and O's route that they hoped would lead them to someone willing to trade their assorted relics and objects for water and medicine. They had said they would journey for a maximum of three days, on the fourth they would turn back, whether they had found anyone or not, and come home.

This morning was the eighth day since they had left.

"So, ye really goin after them then Ast?"

Lizzie walked out from the darkness of the cave, her outfit a chaotic mix of rags and gaffer tape.

"They've been gone too long Liz, and Ruan's ankle isn't getting any better. Max and O should have returned by now. I'll follow their trail and meet them at some point, see if I can gee them along a bit."

"You could wait one more day Ast, they'll be here soon..." Liz took Astrid's hand, her fingers felt warm against the coolness of hers. She squeezed and ran her other fingers across Liz's face, tucking the forever-rebellious brown hair behind Liz's ear.

"Its not that I want to go Liz, Ru is in an awful way, you've seen the infection."

"I know, I'm being selfish, I just ... I just don't fancy being alone tonight."

"I'll be back soon, Max and O are probably just beyond the valley," Astrid kissed Liz then stepped back, tightening the straps of her backpack. It was time to go, delaying leaving was not going to help her or the gang.

"Make Ru comfortable as best you can Liz, get some of the others to recheck the pool in the cave, there might be a little bit of moisture we missed. Just make sure no one else breaks anything in there. Oh and your on sheet duty."

"Fab, thanks captain," Liz threw what appeared to be a salute, "be careful Ast, yeah?"

Astrid walked over and gave Liz a hug then left, tracing the creek bed down into the valley. She paused midway down the creek, turning back to see that Liz was still watching her from the mouth of the cave, Astrid waved farewell and Liz responded before retreating back inside. The plastic sheet now still, sunlight playing across its surface.

Astrid depressed StepMom's [mute] button, re-activating the AI. A squeal of feedback indicated that the unit was kicking into life.

"Morning Steps, can you start scanning for breadcrumbs and any signals from Mother." StepMom began to twitter and whine, complaining about the fact that her batteries had not been recharged correctly. Astrid had to stop herself from automatically hitting the [mute] button, much as StepMom was a pain Astrid needed the AI to find Max's trail.

So she set off whilst StepMom belittled her lack of pace and that searching for the trail was beneath her capabilities.

It was going to be a long walk.

oooooo

The first breadcrumb that StepMom led Astrid to was hidden within the root system of a dead tree that marked the edge of a forest. Astrid peered into the depths between the other burnt sentinels, naked without leaf, undergrowth or birds. The forest seemed to consume the landscape, spreading as far and wide as she could see.

The sun bleached everything turning the world into a mosaic of monochrome shadows and sinister shapes. She hated how the woods made her feel scared, that each tree just reminded her that nothing grew anymore since the war. Astrid replaced the breadcrumb, a small silver nano-cube that would enable her, Max and O to retrace their steps when she had finally found where they had gotten too. The one thing she didn't want to do was go into the woods, yet the AI was insistent that the next nano lay in that direction. Knowing the answer already, she re-checked with the AI for what must have been the fifteenth time.

"Steps, are you absolutely sure?"

"Of course I am! Your Brother located the next breadcrumb 3.4km directly south of our position. I strongly recommend that we proceed."

"Alright, just ... oh, hold on."

Astrid pulled out the In-Viz cloak from the depths of her backpack. As she covered herself, Stepmom and her backpack, she tried to ignore the claustrophobic anxiety that she always felt as the thin nano-plastic enfolded her. From inside the cloak there was little difference to the world but Astrid knew that the cloak's nano-tech was already bending the light, making her nearly invisible. Though she detested wearing the thing because it normally made her sweat, the one thing navigating the wasteland taught you was that you were never alone for long.

As she ventured into the shadows of the dead trees, the dry branches underneath each step cracked like gunshots. She chided herself for her stupidity, what was the point in being invisible if you were then going to make such a racket? She forced herself to focus, watching each step, navigating through the ranks of this wooden graveyard that once would have blocked out the sun with a canopy of green. Now the sky pressed down, without leaf or cloud to break up the glare of the sun. She tried to imagine the forest before the war, a living organism full of emerald shapes and bickering life. How the rain would feel, how it would sound, and taste as it dropped through the leaves. Pattering on the ground underfoot. It wasn't long before she had to stop her imagination, forced to sip some of her precious dirty water, tormented by thirst.

After what felt like an eternity she found the next breadcrumb. Max had concealed it deep within the rotting remains of a fallen tree. Astrid nervously prodded at the hole with a stick, convinced that something would bite her hand if she reached in. But there was nothing, just another cube followed by StepMom's impatient demand that they continue southwards, for she had already located the next crumb, five kilometres south of their position. Though it would be nice, the AI admonished, if Astrid could be bothered to note her efficiency once in a while.

Not for the first time Astrid wished that Max hadn't taken Mother on his expedition. Mother was nice, comforting, supportive. StepMom was just a bitch.

Before long the light began to fail and as reticent as Astrid was to stop she knew, thankfully, a nearby tree had enough space within its roots to accommodate her. Fearful again of what might be living in the depths, Astrid activated StepMom, bathing the interior in a yellow glow. There seemed to be nothing untoward within, no bugs or nasties to eat her alive during the night. Lying on the dry earth, Astrid used her backpack as a pillow and pulled the viz up over her face. There was no sound outside of the tree, just the odd branch falling to earth. Telling StepMom to awaken her if she detected anything approaching her hideout, Astrid allowed her eyes to close and fell asleep within seconds.

The next morning, after a breakfast of brown water and what turned out to be a tin that contained butter beans, Astrid set off towards the next breadcrumb. The woods, like her journey seemed to drag on forever. At least the treasure hunt for the trail was alleviating her bad mood this morning. One crumb was hidden in a small hole waist high in a tree, the next concealed within a few stones stacked together. After that, she tired of the trail, fed up with StepMom's incessant complaints at her lack of pace and how her AI system was designed for more glamorous tasks.

Finally the trees began to thin out, she was nearing the edge of the forest, and before long, Astrid was walking across the dry dust of what, she assumed, was once a field. Normally she hated the sun, but after two days in the oppressive wood, she felt relief at the sense of space and freedom. She followed the contours of the land, pleasantly undulating for a while, but soon it began to climb upwards towards a clump of hills. StepMom's scans detected that the next crumb would be on the other side of the rise, at the base of a valley. The climb up was tiring, the dirt earth sagging under her feet, but soon Astrid had reached the summit. Glad to have a place to rest, Astrid took shelter in the shade of a large stone that seemed to have grown out of the top of the hill, sipping at some of her warm cave water.

From her vantage point she could see a small dwelling down on the other side of the valley below. Through the scratched lens of her binoculars she could make out the smashed windows, assorted graffiti and the front door hanging off of hinges, indicating that the house had been abandoned long ago and probably ransacked several times over.

She double-checked StepMom, but the AI was firm, Astrid had to go to the house.

For the breadcrumb was, without question, somewhere within it.

What was Max thinking? The one rule they had was to steer clear of such places, to give them a wide berth. Astrid scanned the surrounding landscape, but saw nothing aside from the odd dead tree and the undulating brown earth that stretched outward forever. If this was a trap then whoever had set it was waiting within. Yet she knew she had no choice, and Max must have had a reason to go in there. Maybe he had left a note or supplies.

With butterflies rising in her stomach, Astrid began the descent towards the building.

oooooo

The breadcrumb had been hidden in what was once a bedroom. There was no bed anymore, just a floor covered in tin cans, dirty clothing and small crushed vials that would have once held pure water. Astrid found the breadcrumb hidden within a small hole in the floor. No note, nothing. Not even supplies.

"Steps can you trace the next breadcrumb."

The AI screen flickered, "There are no other crumbs within ten kilometres of our current position."

"Can you double check?"

"Why of course, I mean why would you believe that I could make such calculations like I have every other time? No, no, just wait." The AI went silent, the screen flickering yellow, "Right, there are no other signals aside from those we have already found."

So where were Max and O? No note, no markers, nothing to tell her where they had gone from here. Astrid slumped to the floor, dejected. She couldn't return empty handed, yet where could she go, who could she find to help?

She left the bedroom, heading down the haphazard wooden steps to the ground floor. The wall had once held photographs, but now just rows of empty pins studded the surface. The stench of something rotting from the kitchen didn't alleviate her mood. The floor was mercifully clear of rubbish, but most of the appliances and cupboards were gone. All that was left was a table with three chairs and an ancient looking cooker with an even older looking metal kettle resting at an angle on its hob.

Astrid sat down at the table, her fingers tracing the various initials and words carved in the surface. A chaotic blend of names, monikers and swearing that charted those that had passed by. She didn't see a MAX or an O. She felt her eyes beginning to droop, her body suddenly sinking into the resistant surface of the old plastic chair.

Maybe she could sleep, just forty winks.

Astrid suddenly woke up; voices off in the distant had caused StepMom to vibrate with alarm. Astrid quickly pulled on the In-Viz cloak and moved towards the door, but it was too late. The voices were close and heading for the house.

She moved to the furthest corner of the kitchen from the door. Wedging herself between the cooker and the wall. All she could do was hope that the cloak worked enough to conceal her. She soon found out. An old man, his skin tanned and leathered by the sun, walked into the kitchen. He carried an axe, his clothes a haphazard mix of knitwear. His eyes were hidden, obscured by goggles. The cloak was thankfully working for he seemed oblivious to Astrid; she covered her mouth, trying to suppress her anxious breathing.

"Nah, nuffin here, place is bloody empty," the man lay his axe down on the table and settled into the chair that a moment ago Astrid had vacated. His back was to her but she was fearful that he would feel the warmth of where she had just been sat, that he would know someone had been here moments ago.

Thankfully his clothing seemed to be too thick for him to notice. He reached into a small leather bag slung across his shoulder and pulled out a tin can. Astrid watched, her stomach growling loud enough to shake the room, as he battled to open the container with a rusty knife. Finally he succeeded in peeling back the metal and began spearing out small squares of fruit. Before long, the man's fellow scavengers, a young boy and an older woman, appeared with the woman scolding him for starting without them. They sat around the table, the can was passed back and forth until it was empty and dirt-encrusted fingers had wiped out the last remnants of juice. Astrid was hoping that they would leave for her legs were aching from being cramped up, but disappointingly, the old lady reached into a small suitcase and pulled out a deck of cards.

Astrid closed her eyes, allowing her mind to wander off. All she could do right now was wait them out. She was startled out of a particularly nice day dream when the old man slammed his hand down after losing yet another game. It seemed that he had decided it was time for them to move on.

"Shall we take the kettle pops? Might do for tradin' or summat?" the boy asked the old man.

"Ay, why not? Might get something from those tight bastards down at the Common eh?" The man coughed, hacking hard into his hands.

Astrid watched as they readied themselves, then the boy walked towards her to grab the kettle. She pushed herself further back into the corner, fearful that he would spot her. He was close enough that if she reached out, she could touch his leg. As he lifted up the kettle, he gave it a little shake, one of those silly little habits, as if there would be any water inside.

That was when the thin line, nearly invisible, that had been stuck to the base of the vessel went taut and then snapped. A blinding white light filled the room, overwhelming Astrid, consuming every sense of her being. She saw the others drop to the floor; bodies flopping like puppets whose strings had been cut.

Then everything went dark.

oooooo

Astrid opened her eyes, flinching at the light. Her head throbbed, as if she had been hit hard. She was still in the corner, but StepMom, the cloak and her backpack were gone. The scavenger who had gone for the kettle was on the floor in front of her, his eyes open, his mouth gagged and his hands bound behind his back. His fellow scavengers were nowhere to be seen.

He looked up at her, his eyes pleading she assumed, but

there was nothing she could do for either of them, for it seemed her hands and feet were also bound.

Footsteps, heavy boots by the sound, approached the kitchen. The sight of the person nearly made Astrid scream. A mask covered the face, body armour and thick black gloves added to a black jumpsuit. There was some sort of gun strapped to his back, another smaller gun hanging from his belt.

This person was neither a trader nor a scavenger. To Astrid, he looked like a soldier. And from the sounds of activity outside, there were more of them.

The man retrieved an orange cloth bag from a pouch on his belt. At the sight of it, the scavenger began trying to struggle out of his bonds, his face grimacing in panic. The soldier ignored his thrashing protestations, and pulled the orange bag over the boy's head. Immediately the scavenger stopped moving. The soldier tightened the bag around the boy's neck with a drawstring, then seemingly satisfied, hoisted the comatose scavenger, with minimal effort, up onto his shoulder.

Alone, Astrid began to struggle against the plastic cuffs that held her hands and feet together. It was hopeless. She was caught. Two more soldiers walked back into the kitchen, dressed in similar black clothing and carrying weapons like the one before. One went to the kettle, and began rearming the trap that the scavenger had inadvertently set off.

Was that what happened to Max and O? Astrid wondered. Had they been captured just like her?

The other soldier walked towards Astrid, pulling out another orange hood. Astrid thrashed around, feeling tears rolling down her cheeks, "please, no, I was just trying to find my brother, my friends they need water, please I'm begging you don't...."

The world suddenly went orange and Astrid stopped being aware of anything else.

oooooo

Gentle fingers lifted the hood from her head. The orange dreams that had consumed Astrid's sense of self was suddenly gone. Thankfully, there was no ringing headache as

93

it was with the pulse trap. Astrid just felt as if someone had flicked a switch from [OFF] to [ON] within her body.

She was surprised to find her hands and feet unbound, and that she wasn't in a cage as she expected. Instead, she sat on a wooden chair. She looked to her right to see that her belongings, including the viz-cloak and StepMom had been laid neatly out on a polished wooden table. Beyond the table, a long window of clean polished glass looked out over a collection of haphazard buildings enclosed by a high wall. Astrid could make out a couple of black clad soldiers patrolling the perimeter, behind them a crown of dusty brown hills spread out as far as the eye could see.

Then someone coughed politely, and Astrid suddenly realised she wasn't alone.

"Welcome Miss....? Of course, how silly, you had no identification on you, well nonetheless welcome to the Citadel."

Astrid looked back towards the voice. Three people were in front of her behind a large wooden table. Two men and one woman, all dressed in clothing that wasn't stained by dirt and sweat. The man in the middle had been the speaker. He had a jolly face, like Father Christmas. The man to his right was thinner, grey eyes hiding behind grey glasses. The lady was younger looking, and had long brown hair that trailed over her shoulders, lying over her pristine black dress. Behind them on the white wall was a large map; it looked familiar, similar to the one that the Trader had shown them a lifetime ago. However, the map was quickly forgotten when Astrid's eyes moved to the jug of water on the table in front of the three people. Beside it was a simple white bowl filled with ... it couldn't be, could it?

The bowl was stacked with fresh apples, pears, plums and grapes. Things that Astrid had only eaten if she had got lucky with the contents of an unlabelled can. Without realising she was doing it, Astrid pinched the skin hard at her left wrist, but nothing disappeared. The old people, the water and fruit remained in front of her.

"Oh my dear, you aren't dreaming! And may I add my apologies for the manner of your arrival." The woman smiled reassuringly at Astrid. "Though I hope you understand that our security personnel only had our best interests at heart.

Are you able to talk?"

Astrid nodded, her eyes never leaving the water and fruit on the table.

"Oh for God's sake, take something girl." The grey-eyed man pushed a glass towards her. "Really Gabor, I have more pressing concerns than this..." he pointed to Astrid.

"Now, now, Simon... manners. We have a guest. Please ignore my colleague, he has been under some pressure recently, would you care for some fruit?" Father Christmas pushed the bowl towards Astrid.

Astrid watched them, but they seemed content, aside from Mr Grey who kept glancing at his watch, to wait until she had consumed something. She had never felt so thirsty, so hungry and she had to do everything to stop herself lunging toward the table. She took a careful sip, the water tasted amazing, so cold and fresh. When she bit into an apple, she almost cried. The memory of what had been lost through the war rising up against her will.

She was brought back to reality when Father Christmas recommenced his introductions.

"My dear, I am Dr Gergely, the elected mayor of our settlement. My impatient colleague is Simon Hopkins in charge of infrastructure and resources, and finally Emma Dumas, Head of Security. We, for want of a better word, run the Citadel and our very interested in understanding why you and the others were scavenging in the farmhouse on the edge of our territory."

Astrid shook her head, she didn't dare look at them, instead she concentrated on the patterns of light moving through the water within her glass.

The grey man cut in, "So you weren't there, is that it? Our patrol was mistaken?"

"No," Astrid replied. "No I just wasn't with them, they were scavenging, I wasn't."

"So what were you doing, child?" Emma asked.

"Hiding, searching..."

"For what?" Hopkins snapped at her.

"For.... For my brother, we ... I ... I had lost him, I thought he might have been in the house. I meant no harm, I didn't take anything."

Gergely nodded reassuringly. "We are not accusing you of

anything; trust me when I say we are only concerned with your welfare. Now what did your brother look like, how old was he?"

"Blond hair, like me, blue eyes, normal looking. He's seventeen, or close to that anyway."

"Okay, well we can at least check to see if he's here in the Citadel for you." Emma gestured to someone, that until then Astrid hadn't realised was in the room. A young man, dressed in a uniform similar to that of the soldiers, stepped up to the table. He looked no older than Max.

"Yes Ma'am?"

"Alex, be a darling will you? Go and check the patrol manifest for the past week or so, see if anyone was picked up that might be...?" She looked inquisitively over towards Astrid.

Astrid paused, she was reluctant to give away too much, "Astrid."

"That might be Astrid's brother, let me know if anything turns up."

Alex nodded and left the four of them. Astrid helped herself to another glass of water. The conversation quickly turned to an informal interrogation. Why was she there? Who else was she with? Were there others?

Astrid answered the first two, but the third she kept the truth to herself. She didn't know these people nor trust them. Not yet. What their intentions were, what they would do to Liz and the others. Well she needed to be sure. If they had Max already, then there was no point in lying about her search for him.

Finally, the questions stopped. The panel, it seemed, was satisfied with her answers. The grey man left abruptly muttering something about output and filter degradation. Dr Gergely warmly welcomed Astrid to Citadel once more and bade goodnight. It just left her with Emma who smiled at Astrid and stood up indicating that she should follow.

"So you must be incredibly tired. We'll wait on Alex for an update regarding your brother, but these things take time. If you want, you are welcome to stay with us. We've had a room prepared for you upstairs. Nothing palatial, sadly, but you should be able to get a decent rest."

"I ... I don't want to impose." Astrid was anxious, she

needed sleep, but felt unsure as to whether she could trust people who had knocked her out twice in one day.

"Astrid, we've all been out there, you know, in the wastelands. This, the Citadel, is rare, precious and needs protection, but all our welcome here; all of us can contribute to a life without thirst and illness. Come, see what the room is like. If you don't like it, you are welcome to leave. Oh and don't forget your things. I'm sorry to say your AI box seems to have stopped functioning, but I'm sure our tech guys can sort that out for you tomorrow.'

Astrid grabbed her belongings in a bundle and followed Emma along a white corridor, all clean and lacking the normal collection of debris. As they climbed up a staircase at the end of the corridor, Astrid could see out a window. A group of children playing in the road, as adults went about tending plants growing within long plastic tunnels. It all looked so normal, so safe.

Emma looked back to see her gazing out over the settlement. "Yes, life is good here. Maybe your brother is out there right now. Hopefully Alex will let us know soon. There aren't more of you are there?"

Astrid looked away from the window and shook her head, Emma turned and the pair began to ascend the stairs.

"Pity, one of our guards mentioned that you shouted something about friends. I'm sure it was the confusion, the aftermath of the pulse. Ah, here we are."

Emma opened a plain wooden door. Inside the room was minimalist, but to Astrid who had spent most of her life in caves and tents, it was an opulent paradise. A small wooden bed, dressed in clean white sheets, a window overlooking the Citadel, a table with some fruit. She was surprised to even see a small sink in the corner with a large jug of water. Emma took a hanger off the back of the door, and handed over a small black overall that looked the right size for Astrid.

"Sorry about the clothing. Not really suitable for a young girl, but it's a lot cleaner than your current ensemble. Now, there's a button just here by the door, feel free to press it if you need anything or have any questions."

"Thank you, I don't know what to say ... or why you would...."

"Astrid, please it's our pleasure. We need new people. We need fresh blood. We need you. Now rest. Hopefully tomorrow we can reunite you with your brother."

Emma left. Astrid stood looking at herself in the mirror. She was shocked to see what she looked like, how old she had gotten. She undressed, glad to be out of her dirty and tired clothing, and slowly washed, watching the water in the sink turn deep rusty brown. When she dressed, the overalls felt like new skin. She sat on her bed watching orange lights flicker into life across the Citadel as night drew in, letting the juice of an incredibly ripe pear spill over her knuckles. The sound of laughter and chatter fluttered on the breeze. Astrid felt her anxiety slip away. The sense of excitement at being safe, being fed and clean overcoming her paranoia.

Maybe she had found Oasis after all. Yet she needed to be sure; she couldn't let Liz and the others down.

Astrid pulled on her In-Viz cloak and tried the door handle. It was unlocked. Tentatively she walked back down the short corridor to the flight of steps. The building seemed deserted, though. As she descended, Astrid braced herself for someone to call out, for an alarm to be raised. Yet she was only greeted by silence. She retraced her way past the room she had met the council in, the bowl of fruit and water still on the table, and made her way until the corridor ended at an ornately carved black wooden door. Nervously, Astrid reached out and took hold of the large brass handle. It felt cold in her hand. Carefully, Astrid turned the handle, expecting it to be locked.

Instead, the door swung open. She stepped out into the street. The road was empty, the children and adults returned to their homes. No screams, no pleas for water, just the strange sound of people living without fear. She walked towards the plastic tunnels that earlier in the day the adults had been working within. They were full with vibrant green plants, bursting with different produce. The aroma and scents inside the tunnel were intoxicating. Astrid plunged her hands into the dark, cool earth. In this place, nature was alive.

She walked back and slipped back inside the council chamber, closing the door behind her. By the time she had returned to her room, she had made up her mind. This was no prison, she could leave, go anywhere, talk to anyone. For the first time in a long time she felt safe.

She pressed the button that Emma had said would summon an aide. Soon, she could hear the main door open and the sound of boots ascending the stairs. A tentative knocking, and in walked a young girl, dressed in black and similar in age to Lizzie.

"You need something Miss?"

"This place, how long have you been here?"

"About three years. My parents were killed, and I ended up here, traded by some bloke at the Commons. Best thing that ever happened to me to be honest. I mean, there's water, an underground reservoir, so big that the Doc, sorry the Mayor, reckons that it'll never run out."

Astrid took a sip of water. She needed to take care of Liz and the others. "I have some friends north of the woods. They're currently taking refuge in a cave. We have a trail of nanos; the first is in the farmhouse I was found in. If you follow it, you'll find them. They need to come here. They're hungry, sick, and thirsty. Ruan has a broken ankle ..." Astrid started to weep, her body shuddering uncontrollably against her will.

"Please Miss, it's okay. I'll let the recon patrol guys know. They'll go get your friends for you. You need to rest up, get some strength back, you'll need it."

The aide departed and Astrid lay down on the bed. She felt exhausted, broken, but relieved. Soon the rest of them would be here, they could be together, maybe they could get their own house, grow fruit, splash in water. As the sounds of the Citadel at night floated in through her open window, Astrid closed her eyes, taking pleasure in the simple delight of lying on a bed. That was when the door burst open, and the aide and a solider entered the room, swiftly crossing toward her. Astrid, confused, sat up, in time to see the aide had an orange hood in her hand.

oooooo

The removal of the orange hood woke Astrid out of her sedation. She lifted her head from her chest, her neck sore. It felt like she needed all her strength just to raise her eyes level. She felt odd, weightless, drained of energy. Though there was little light her eyes slowly adjusted to the gloom. Her hands were shackled to a steel frame that was clamped to a wall. Her feet were also strapped, and a thick belt looped around her waist. Whoever else was in the room, Astrid couldn't tell. For in front of her and to both sides hung thick sheets of plastic.

A hacking cough off to her right broke through the silence. Astrid tried to see through the plastic but all she could see was a shadow.

"Who's there?"

"Just me and your friends, Astrid." The plastic sheet in front of her was pulled aside, white light forced Astrid's eyes to clamp shut, her hands flinching to shield her face, but held by the restraints.

Gingerly, Astrid opened her eyes. Squinting with the light, the silhouette in front of her slowly blurred into focus. It was the grey man.

"Mr Hopkins? What - where am I?"

"Where you wanted to be Astrid, with your brother. If I may..."

Mr Hopkins stepped over and pulled back the sheet that was hanging to Astrid's right. The shadowy figure, though thin and emaciated, was familiar. It was Max. He was strapped to another steel frame, suspended off of the ground. Max's head was lolling, as if he was dreaming. She was shocked to see that various thick tubes ran in and out of Max's torso. From her position, Astrid could see two in particular: one full of red blood, another seemed to be filled with a dirty fluid.

Mr Hopkins let the sheet go. Max was once more nothing but a shadow. Astrid looked down, unable to look Hopkins in the eye, and was shocked to see similar tubes protruding from her body. Water pulsing inwards, blood slowly seeping outwards.

Astrid started to scream, to weakly thrash, she yelled out for her brother, for help, for anyone. She screamed until she felt too weak, too overwhelmed, to continue. The whole time Hopkins just studied her, like a collector examining a prize butterfly.

"No one can hear you, nor will they help you if they did."

Hopkins adjusted a tube coming out of Astrid's arm, squeezing it until a sludgy brown material started slowly moving into her body. "You are now a resident in what we call the Works, an integral part of our community."

"I don't...." Astrid felt even weaker, as if the brown sludge was slowly forcing her asleep. Hopkins seemed unconcerned, talking to himself, as much as her, as he checked her pulse and then her pupils.

"You see we had a dilemma. We found the underground reservoir with enough water for a thousand lifetimes. I'm sure you could understand our dismay when we realised that, like most things, the war had contaminated it. Our chance at existence turned undrinkable, totally worthless, irradiated filth. Some did try to drink it, in the early days; their deaths were particularly unpleasant.

"Then, well I'm not one to boast, but I worked out a way of filtering the water, making it safe to drink. You see, the human body is quite an incredible device, very adaptable and resilient. One of those tubes connects you to the reservoir. Ah, good, it seems the sedatives are finally taking affect."

Hopkins lifted her face up from her chest, looking into her eyes, brushing some hair away from her mouth. Then gently lowered it back down.

"Yes, so what happens, in layman's terms, is that the nasty water goes in, your body processes it, and clean safe water manifests as part of your blood system. 90% of your blood is water, you see. We then draw out just enough of the old red stuff so as not to kill you. Then your blood is subsequently processed, and we separate the water content out from the other bits. Bingo! Clean drinkable water for our little community, and the rest of the blood gets used as fertilizer for our plants. All we need to do is keep you dosed and fed, and you should be able to work for at least two months, if not more. A very efficient system if you don't mind me saying."

Astrid could barely hear him now, the world was slowly slipping into shadows. Hopkins leant in close, whispering into her ear.

"It is a shame that you filters have a limited life span. Though you may find solace in knowing that when your time comes, your body will be transformed into fuel for the rest of your fellow workers. So every cloud has a silver lining, eh?

"Now I should go. It was nice to meet you Astrid. I'll leave you to catch up with your sibling."

Whether Hopkins cared or not, Astrid was oblivious to his departure. Her eyes didn't even register when the lights were turned off, plunging her back into darkness. She was lost in another world now, one in which she and Max played within the crystal waters of a magnificent fountain. Splashing each other and laughing, as jets of water arched across a blue sky filled with white clouds.

About Andrew Patch

Andrew's fiction has featured in, amongst others, *Firewords Quarterly*, *With Painted Words*, *The Were Traveler* and the drabble anthology *100 Worlds*. He is currently working on a sci-fi novel set in England during the 1990s.

Occasionally he writes things on Twitter: @imageronin

The Rumpled Man

by Setsu Uzume

The snow sizzled against the translucent blue dome. Birds sometimes met the same fate, evidenced by the putrefying carcasses just a few inches from the base. It was meant to keep out all kinds of things—insects, predators, pathogens. Sometimes it identified snowflakes as equally insidious.

Lyolee and Margret often wriggled through the piles of broken cars, torn plastic bags, and gutted apartments to sit by the edge of the dome and watch what happened when things tried to cross through it. They especially enjoyed it when a rat or a seagull got too close.

On this January day, they watched a rat skitter toward the edge of the dome. The electrified blue field was flush with the ground—no way under or over. The rat skittered close, and sniffed a blade of grass. It sniffed the metal panel near the edge of the dome, and skittered closer. The girls' eyes bulged as they watched it, grins widening—when a tiny arc of electric death popped from the surface of the dome and tagged the rat. It shrieked, jumped into the air, and then fell to the ground.

Margret always covered her face with both hands and giggled when she saw it twitch.

"C'mon let's go," said Lyolee.

"Why?" said Margret. "We just got here."

"I want to get a snack," said Lyolee. "I promised Dee we'd meet him there."

"Ew," said Margret.

"Oh shut up," said Lyolee. She got up and crawled over half a porcelain tub. Margret followed her.

They clambered over the mountains of garbage for another ten minutes before they hopped down off an engine and landed on concrete. They heard a piano in the distance.

"Dammit, it's started already," said Margret. There was a swarm of people at the gate. The market was open.

Lyolee ran through the crowds of grown-ups. Hawkers, peddlers, suits and junkies all ignored the girls as they ran past. They may as well have been stray dogs.

A dingy flag with yellowed letters hung between torn scraps of chain-link fence. It read "Armer's Market" to recall the olden days.

Margret loved the Armer's Market. Everyone from the lowlands gathered into the city. They traveled hours and hours by foot, hauling carts of scrap metal and corrugated fiberglass, or even—treasure of all treasures—edible greens so delicate they lay limp as hair on the wooden tables. Margret always stopped to get a whiff of them, just a whiff before the hauler smacked her upside the head and told her to keep her grubby fingers away from his wares.

All the riches of the dome were there for the city to enjoy. It was amazing how the Upward Cycle could create such wonders from devastation.

"C'mere!" hissed Lyolee, tugging Margret's jacket.

Dee stood behind a piano in the center of the Market, keeping time on the low keys while an older boy tapped out a tune for the milling crowd. Lyolee dragged Margret back behind a cart. The two of them watched Dee and the older boy play the piano together, in the circle of stones in the center of the square. Folks swerved around them. They dropped money, or heckled, as the two kept playing in their own little dome.

"Don't *lean*, he'll see you!" said Lyolee.

Margret pulled her arm back from Lyolee's grip. "So what? You started it."

"He's really good, isn't he?" She said.

Margret glanced back at Dee. Lyolee was always talking about him. The way he looked, the way he talked, the way he played.

Margret eyed a cart with a lowered awning over it. The tent flaps brushed the ground. She didn't recognize it from the other markets. You had to know which sellers were mean, and which ones would look the other way if you stole a bite.

Margret left Lyolee where she was, and wandered over.

It was dark inside. There was a small carpeted space for customers to walk around, surrounded by three tables. The first table on her left held an array of stones and pebbles. The second table, to her right, had a bunch of little metal trinkets—broken forks and pipes that had moved upward in the Cycle to become objects of beauty rather than objects of use.

The third table...oh, the third table. There were all kinds of things laid out on soft purple fabric. Boxes. Complicated spring contraptions. Yellow metal and silver polished so brightly Margret could see herself in them.

"Hello, young miss," said the man perched behind the third table.

Margret hadn't noticed him in the gloom behind the shining trinkets. He looked old. His clothes were thick and rumpled. He wore a headscarf that covered his forehead almost to the eyebrows. His skin stretched tight across his cheekbones and made his eyes bright. Repulsive was the wrong word. His face drew attention to itself—but handsome wasn't the right word either.

"Hello," Margret said.

"Did you lose your way?" said the Rumpled Man.

"No, I wanted to ask you..." Margret glanced back at the glittering tools. A notched spoon for measuring. A knife with files and screwdrivers that stuck out like extra arms. Her eye lingered on a tiny box, turquoise, with little mirrors inlaid on the top and sides. "Why is your booth covered?" she asked.

The Rumpled Man stared down at Margret as though she were a sniffing rat. She shrank back. No one ever paid more attention to her than it took to shoo her away.

"The light is bad," said the Rumpled Man. "You shouldn't sit out in it. It's pretty while it shines, but it'll rot your skin. Cancer, young miss. Gotta be careful."

"What's in that jar?" asked Margret, pointing to a vial of what looked like brown noses chopped from the faces of men.

"It's the Divine Cap, grown from filth, but when eaten, you see beyond this world," said the Rumpled Man.

"What's that?" asked Margret, pointing at a walking stick with a gold ring and necklace hammered into it.

"A more ambitious project," said the Rumpled Man.

"That's not very interesting," said Margret. "What have you *really* got?"

The Rumpled Man nodded once, then turned and opened a tiny door in the cart. As soon as both of his hands were busy, Margret snatched the mirrored box and slipped away.

A sweet seller was bending to hand treats to Lyolee and Dee. "One for Lyolee, and one for Dee," he said. Then he turned to Margret. "What's your name, sweetheart?"

Margret tugged both of their elbows. "Gotta jam," she said.

The three of them trotted out of the Armer's Market. They had almost reached the entrance when they heard a policeman shout. "You three! Stop!"

The three children broke into a run. They wove through the legs of slow-moving shoppers and dodged around a bicycle. They heard the policeman coming up behind them, shouting for them to stop and blowing his whistle.

They ran and ran. They made it across the streets back to their part of the city—where they could disappear into the nooks and crannies like mice.

"What did you get?" asked Lyolee. Dee scooted up next to her, panting, with a big grin on his face.

Margret took the box out of her shirt. They'd never seen anything as bright and vivid as the turquoise box. Tiny mirrors sparkled and lit up their faces.

"There's something written on it," said Margret.

"Lemme see, Lyolee," said Dee.

Lyolee held the box out to him, and he took it. He turned the box over. The flowing letters were inlaid with gold leaf. "It says... *Tell me your name, and open me bold, I'll transform your dream into coins of gold.*"

"Huh," said Lyolee, taking it back from him. "Think there's gold inside?" She fiddled with the box a moment, and then found the seam where the box met the lid. No sooner did she pry it open, she disappeared. The other two jumped back in alarm.

The box clinked to the concrete and snapped shut.

Margret and Dee looked at each other, then at the box.

"Lyolee?" called Margret.

"Lyolee!" called Dee. They looked around, but there was no sign of her. Margret swore.

"What did you do?" asked Dee, kicking the box. It bounced off a brick wall and spun back toward them.

"Nothing! This isn't *my* fault!" said Margret. She bent and scooped up the box, brushing dirt off it.

"We've got to get help!" Dee screamed. Margret knew what he was thinking. Maybe Lyolee had been snatched.

"We can't go to the cops, Dee, don't be stupid!" said Margret.

Dee shook his head, took a step back, and ran toward the eastern sector—to the police.

He's so dumb, she thought. *They won't be able to help us.* Margret shoved the box into her shirt pocket. No sense wasting it —she'd pawn it off later that night when the shops are ready to close. She took off after him.

Dee's long legs carried him faster than Margret could match. They wove around adults and proper families, and shouts follow them. *Watch where you're going! Disgusting! Rotten kids!* Dee didn't slow down at the road even though the light was against him. Margret rounded a corner just as Dee entered the street. He took six long strides, and a sooty yellow car slammed its brakes.

Bang!

Dee's body rolled—a limp and boneless doll. He came to a stop over a sewer, and black ooze began spreading from his head and chest.

The cars kept moving until the policeman arrived. For him, they stopped.

"You there! Did you see what happened? What's your name?" he shouted, advancing on Margret. Behind the policeman, on the other side of the street, Margret saw the Rumpled Man.

The Rumpled Man considered her with a frown. Then he looked at Dee's body in the road. He drew a square in the air with two fingers, and took a similar box from his pocket. He raises his eyebrows significantly, and flips the box over.

The policeman was getting closer. He kept asking Margret her name. She didn't want to disappear. All the kids that the cops took were never seen again. *Go, go, go!* Margret screamed to herself. She slapped the policeman's outstretched hand away, and ran for the junkyard.

She ran for a long time. Panting, she ducked into an alleyway. She took out the box and looked at it. The Rumpled Man's face leapt to mind, and she shuddered. She flipped the box over. On the underside of the box there were the same flowing letters, but in black rather than gold. It took her several minutes to sound out the words:

Call me nothing, name me true; steal from me I'll take from you.

A creaky old voice drifted over from the other side of the ally. "Guess my name and you'll get your friend back."

Margret squeezed the box in her hand. "Did you kill Dee? Was that your fault?"

The Rumpled Man folded his arms and looked at her. "You've already gotten what you wanted. Guess my name, or I'll keep your friend as payment."

"Victor."

The Rumpled Man smiled, but shook his head.

Against her better judgment, Margret decided to play along. "Taylor, Peter, Jack, Thomas, Vinny, Trey, Liwei!" She shouted. "Ralphie, Andre, Matt, Tyrone, Eric, David, Jay!"

The Rumpled Man just grinned at her.

Margret fumed, daring to step toward him. "Snitch, pansy, pizza-face, jerk, idiot, stalker! Moron, sissy, weirdo, freak, stupid psycho creeper!"

The Rumpled Man lifted his chin and stroked it. "Thief," he said.

Margret was too angry to be scared. She ran, leapt and tackled the Rumpled Man. He fell back. The two of them wrestled. He reached into her shirt to retrieve the box.

"Give me back my friends!" she screamed. "Give them back and you can have your stupid box!"

The Rumpled Man yanked the box from Margret's hands. She clamped her hands over his to stop him. As he looked down at her, his face twisted into a putrid smile. He opened the box, and disappeared.

The box clinked to the concrete, and snapped shut.

Margret screamed. She picked up the box and pounded it into the street. After a few minutes, she sat quietly as tears poured from her eyes.

Should I open it? Suppose I become a prisoner. There's got to be another way.

Names were how they found you. Names were how they got you. She couldn't go to the police. She had to find Lyolee herself.

All that night Margret ran through the city looking for Lyolee. She went to the children's shelter. She went to the shops and the alleys where they usually looked for food. She went to the gates of High Nob but couldn't risk asking the guards. She asked other kids if they'd seen her. She looked and looked until the blue dome's flickering light faded against the sky. Dawn.

She wandered over the junk from the old time and sat at their spot. At this time, yesterday, she and Lyolee had sat and watched the rats die. They had watched the seagulls die. Before Dee died, they had laughed.

Margret sniffed and pulled the box out of her pocket. She turned it over in her hands, and re-read the inscription. The wind kicked up snowflakes and they sizzled against the dome while she steeled herself. She found the seam where the box met the lid, and tugged.

She tugged again. It was stuck. Dented and bent so that it couldn't open, even though the little mirrors didn't have a scratch.

Margret slapped a tear from her face and stood, snarling.

She hurled the box at the dome. It flashed and popped with electricity as sailed right through.

She heard a gentle tap.

The billowing snow thinned, and a gnarled hand held the box aloft. Bony fingers curled around it. Then there was a gentle *crunch... crunch... crunch* of footsteps breaking the snow's crust.

The Rumpled Man stood next to his cart on a snowdrift far outside the dome. There was another figure out there. The wind died down, and Margret squinted through her tears.

It was Lyolee. She was outside the dome. She trudged through the snow toward the barren junkyard. Margret shrieked and ran toward her, stopping short of the electric field.

"Lyolee?"

Lyolee staggered to the left, and looked around. Her jaw hung slack, and her sunken eyes didn't seem to focus on anything. Her breath came in short, quick gasps. Even with the dome between them, her skin looked blue and frostbitten.

Margret waved her arms and shouted, "Lyolee, *don't!*"

At the sound, Lyolee turned toward Margret and slammed face-first into the barrier. Electric arcs exploded all around her.

Margret crashed backward onto a pile of rusted grates. Lyolee hit the snow with a soft thump. After a moment or two, only Margret got up.

She crawled toward her friend, reaching for her, but afraid to go near the dome again.

Snowflakes sizzled against the barrier, or came to rest on Lyolee's body without any sound at all.

Margret whispered her friend's name. It was all that was left of her.

Margret locked eyes with the Rumpled Man. The snow whirled around him. He nodded once, and walked into the blizzard, his cart creaking behind him.

About Setsu Uzume

Setsu Uzume is a novelist and regular contributor to *Art Animal* magazine. She co-founded both Write Club Seattle and Write City San Francisco, where new writers can take their first steps toward publication. Setsu has dabbled in many arts, but only martial arts and writing seem to have stuck. She is represented by Larsen-Pomada Literary Agency. For more of her work, please visit KatanaPen.Wordpress.com.

Beware: Here Be DRAGONS

by Sara Opalka

I ran into an abandoned store, slamming the door behind me with a force that almost knocked it off its rusted hinges. I didn't even have the luxury of taking a second to catch my breath before I was scrambling through the maze of overturned shelves and hazardous soup cans littering the floor. Behind me, the front door was blown apart with a deafening bang that lifted me off my feet and threw me to the ground. I had run out of time.

The DRAGONS were here.

A person who lived before the fall of the old government would have scoffed if they heard that dragons were chasing me. But I knew better. I wasn't facing an oversized green lizard with a persuasion towards kidnapping princesses and duelling with knights. I was facing DRAGONS.

Destructive **R**econnaissance **A**rtificial **G**rade **O**mnipresent **N**octurnal **S**eekers.

The only thing the two had in common was that the crazy person who invented those scary robots had gone to a lot of trouble to come up with a viable acronym.

Oh, and they breathed fire as well.

In my world, the new world, no one wanted to be trapped anywhere with DRAGONS. They were surprisingly deceptive. They looked like floating metal spheres to the naked eye. I don't think anyone besides their creator had ever gotten close enough to one to see its flamethrower or laser section. I didn't give them a chance to use them; I was up and out of the back door before they could complete a scan of the store.

I ran down the alleyway, practically throwing my exhausted body over the wire fence at the end. I heard another bang from behind me; it was most likely the back door being blown to smithereens. I didn't look back, just kept running.

I emerged onto a street, littered with the hollow shells of cars. I sneaked a peek behind me to see that the DRAGONS had just rounded the corner but were being slowed down by their scanners. I had a few things working in my favour. The DRAGONS were machines, which meant they were precise. They didn't work on adrenaline like I was, they first had to examine their surroundings and determine the best course of action. The other thing in my favour was the reason behind the N in their name. They were solar powered and spent all day charging so they could hunt through the night. And I could see the first rays of sunlight seeping over the horizon. They would be nearly out of juice. Never had I been more grateful to see a sunrise.

I ducked behind one of the rusted cars and peered out through a broken window. The DRAGONS were giving up their pursuit and leaving. I was safe.

I slumped to the ground, too exhausted to do a victory dance.

"Impressive," said a voice to my right.

I jumped so high in the air; I was surprised I wasn't sucked into the sun. I shakily pulled out my hunting knife, brandishing it in front of me.

A guy was sitting next to me, with chestnut brown hair and green eyes. He had an easy smile and raised eyebrows. A black and white border collie sat beside him, it wagged its bushy tail and woofed quietly at me.

I let out a breath. "If you're going to kill me, just get it over with. I've stopped caring at this point."

His grin widened. "Killing you requires effort. I could have just let the DRAGONS have you."

"Gee, thanks."

He winked. "Anytime."

I got to my feet, my muscles protesting. "Nice chatting with you, but you know, places to go, people to see."

His grin faded as he jumped to his feet, "Hey, wait. I didn't mean to startle you. I'm Jason by the way."

He held out his hand for me to shake, but I ignored him and started walking away. "That's nice."

"Come on." He was suddenly beside me, his long legs easily keeping up. "I know we just met and all but I was wondering if you wanted to grab dinner with me sometime?"

That threw me. I stopped and raised an eyebrow at him, "Are you serious? A date? Have you seen the world lately? There aren't restaurants anymore! Last week I ate food from a trash bin and I never thought I would say this, but I don't think you can compete with that."

I started walking again and this time he didn't follow.

"At least tell me your name!"

I gave him one last look before I turned a street corner. "I'm sorry but my mother told me not to talk to strangers."

I couldn't help but notice that he was grinning despite my coldness toward him.

oooooo

That afternoon, I woke from an unrestful sleep. I was holed up in the attic of an old house. The occupants were long gone and it was one of the many hideouts I stored supplies in. I couldn't stop thinking about the DRAGONS.

Ok, maybe not just the DRAGONS. That guy was just so... confident. I had just been running for my life, was exhausted, bleeding and bruised, sweaty and my hair was practically in dreadlocks and he had asked be out on a DATE. Who does that?

I ran my fingers through my long auburn hair, not surprised at its poor condition. God, I needed a shower. And a fresh change of clothes. And while I'm at, a time machine would be nice. That way I could go back before the world went to hell. Before a crazy guy with a huge bank account, innumerable destructive weapons and way too much overcompensation had decided that world domination was his destiny.

And did I mention this lunatic happened to be in love with me?

That's right, little old me was the object of this crazy guy's delusions.

I'll be the first to admit I wasn't the best person, back before. I was a "daddy's little princess" type, waited on hand and foot. My father owned a lot of companies, I never really paid attention to what they were, just the fact that they made him, and therefore me, a lot of money. I used to model in my spare time; all the big brands wanted me. That was before I had a scar running down my face from my eyebrow to my lips. The blade of my attacker had just missed my eye. I now kept my hair down all the time, and I was no longer anybody's princess. I had learnt very quickly, that in this world the only person I could rely on was me.

I unpacked my supply bag, mentally taking stock of what was left. Three cans of unidentifiable food, it was a lucky dip when the labels peeled off, two bottles of water, a flashlight, batteries, a Swiss army knife, clothes, aspirin, bandages, a can opener, matches, a pen and some protein bars. I was going to need to find some more supplies soon.

Now normally I don't condone stealing, but when the apocalypse has been and gone and what's left is not enough for those who survived, it's a necessity. I've robbed more people than I can count, but I always made sure I wasn't taking from those who desperately needed it. I guess I was kind of like Robin Hood, in a way, except I only gave to myself.

I packed up my gear and left the house, it was time to leave town. The DRAGONS were getting too close for me to remain here any longer. It wasn't them I was afraid of, but their master. That crazy lunatic who was stalking me? His name is Lucas and he invented them to find me.

And bring me back to him.

Like hell that was going to happen.

oooooo

Before I left town, I stopped at what used to be a computer warehouse. There was this older guy who lived there, his name was Malcolm, but I always thought of him as a wizard with technology. I was hoping he might know something about DRAGONS weaknesses, if they even had any. Before the world went crazy, Malcolm was one of those live-in-his-mother's-basement type of guys, who played *World of Warcraft* every waking minute and knew more about computers than the guy who invented them. He was a bit scatterbrained and didn't interact with people as well as he did with machines. I heard from another survivor that if anyone could find a way to defeat the DRAGONS, it would be him.

I entered the back of the store, knowing that the front was boarded up. I did a secret knock on the door, it was something from a popular movie but I could never remember which one. I heard the rattle and scraping of more than a necessary amount of locks being undone before the door was opened an inch and Malcolm poked his head out.

"Gwen? Is that you? What are you doing here?"

I rolled my eyes, "Do you also remember how you told me to come see you about the DRAGONS?"

Malcolm pondered that for a moment, using a dirty fingernail to scratch his balding head, "It does sound like something I might say. Well, come on in then, before someone sees you."

I suppressed the urge to roll my eyes again, I always forgot how much Malcolm was able to get on my nerves.

I walked into Malcolm's workshop, ignoring the echo of Malcolm scraping and rattling the locks back into place. As usual, there were wires, pieces of hardware and scraps of unidentifiable metal on every available surface. Malcolm once claimed that he had it "in an order" but it was obviously not one known to man. I heard Malcolm mumbling to himself as he walked past me and made his way to a work bench in the centre of the room. I approached it, thinking that the round metal object on the bench looked familiar.

"Damn Malcolm!" I yelled when I recognised it, hurriedly booking it back out of the room. "You brought a damn DRAGON in here?"

He shook his head at me as if I were five years old. "It's deactivated. Harmless."

"You wouldn't think it was so harmless if you had seen one in action," I muttered. I took a deep breath and slowly approached the robot, half expecting it to wake up from its mechanical slumber and decide to attack me.

Malcolm ignored me and went back to examining its insides. I could see half of the outer shell had been gutted and was lying all over the bench.

"Where did you get one?" I asked.

"Some guy brought it in to me, said he brought it down with a high powered rifle and some clever timing," Malcolm replied, pulling more of the wires out of the dead machine.

I whistled. That guy must have been pretty good. The little death machines were notoriously hard to take out. It was far easier to run away and live to fight another day.

"So what have you found out about it?"

"Less than I would have if some people didn't stop asking me stupid questions," Malcolm said.

I gave him a death glare but he didn't notice. He never did. I watched for a few more minutes as Malcolm examined a certain component or wrote down notes in a ragged notebook. After what seemed like a thousand years, Malcolm finally remembered I was there and looked up from his work. "These are very sophisticated. The chip inside them is next generation technology, definitely not something you could buy from any old store. They are programmed with very few directives, but they are almost impossible to sway from them. Lucas is one very smart, very crazy guy."

"But do they have any weaknesses?" I asked impatiently.

"Aside from their need to recharge their solar batteries every day? None that I've found yet. But I only got this two days ago, I need more time to work on it."

I huffed, "I might not have two days, Malcolm! Lucas wants me and you know how obsessive he can be."

Malcolm pulled off his glasses to wipe them on his stained shirt. "I don't know what you want me to say. I'm not a miracle worker. I can't conjure up a magical solution. The best I can do for you is give you a low grade frequency disrupter that might mess with their scanners long enough to give you a chance to get away."

I sighed. It was better than nothing.

"Thanks, Malcolm."

oooooo

Dusk was beginning to darken the sky, and I knew it was time to find a place to hide out. I was about five hours out of town and pretty sure the DRAGONS wouldn't be able to find me easily. My feet were sore, and I hadn't stopped to rest for fear of losing daylight. I needed sleep, but was too keyed up to be able to settle down enough for that. I got off the highway and turned into a farm I spotted from the road. It was set back far enough to not be easily visible and was only surrounded by farmland, dead earth and weeds. I made it to the main house before the sun had completely set and checked the house for occupants. When I was sure it was clear I bedded down in the large rust coloured barn at the back of the property. I noticed a few horses in the paddock that were able to survive on the leftover vegetation and creek running through the property. I guess they didn't want to stray too far from home.

I found some blankets in the cellar of the house, and along with some jars of dried vegetables and some salted meats, was able to have what I considered in the new world to be a feast. I curled up in my blankets but knew I would not be sleeping; I had to be vigilant tonight.

A loud snap brought me out of my thoughts, and I scrambled to my feet, knees shaking, and knife at the ready. If the DRAGONS had found me, they would not be taking me alive. I was getting tired of running.

I silently padded to the barn doors and opened one, wincing when it squeaked so loud there was no way someone could not have heard. I couldn't see anything in the darkness, not even the tell-tale red beams of the DRAGONS' scanners.

A black and white dog emerged from the darkness and ran up to me, tongue out, tail wagging. I was too stunned to react at first, His owner, Jason, materialised a moment later, grinning like the cat that got the cream.

"What do you want?" I asked, clutching my knife as if it were a shield.

"Whoa there," he said putting his hands out as if he were approaching a wild animal. "I'm not going to hurt you; we were just passing through and thought we would stay at this place tonight."

"We?" I asked.

"Yeah, me and Jasper," he said, nodding at the dog who was sniffing me curiously.

117

"Oh," I said, "Well, you can't stay here."

"Come on," he said with a cocky smile, stalking closer, "Please? Just for one night."

"No," I replied, taking a step back, "You need to leave."

I heard myself saying the words but my heart was beating loudly and my breaths were quick. Jason continued inching forward and I kept going back until I hit the barn wall. Crap! I thought, where's the door?

"It's ok," Jason said, "Do you want to put down the knife?"

"No," I replied shakily. Jason was a foot away, I could see into his deep emerald green eyes. He had a strong jaw and his hair was shaggy and a little long.

He smiled at my continued stubbornness, "Ok then, but I bet your arm's gonna get sore pretty soon."

"It's fine."

"Sure." He said, clearly not believing me. "I guess if that's the way you feel, we'll get going." He whistled for his dog.

I should have been happy he was leaving but a part of me wanted him to stay. I'll admit it, I was lonely. I hadn't really spoken to anyone in months; I was always running and leaving town before I could get to know anyone. And, I thought, if the DRAGONS came tonight, there would be someone else to help me against them.

"Wait," I said as he turned away.

Jason turned back around, smiling already. God, my insides were melting from that smile. Why did he have to be so good looking on top of it all?

I looked anywhere but at him, "I guess there's enough room in the barn for both of us. And your dog." I tried not to let him see the heat creeping into my face.

"Thanks," he said and I followed him into the barn, wondering if I had made a mistake.

oooooo

I settled down in my corner of the barn, once again wrapped in my blankets. But this time my hunting knife lay in easy reach. Jason had unpacked his sleeping gear in the opposite corner and Jasper was busy sniffing every inch of the building.

"So," Jason said conversationally, "You never did tell me what your name is."

"No," I replied, "I didn't."

"Why were the DRAGONS after you?"

"Why do you ask so many questions?"

Ok, I was a little grumpy. I was tired.

Jason came and sat down beside me, but just out of reach of my knife. "Look," he said, running his hand through his shaggy hair, "I realise we're practically strangers and we only met the other day but I just want to get to know you. I haven't talked to another human in quite a while."

He watched Jasper sniffing in the corner and I felt like I was really seeing him for the first time. I sighed, I knew exactly what it was like to be lonely.

"At least you have your dog," I said.

He smiled, but it didn't reach his eyes this time, "Yeah," he said softly.

My heart wrenched a little at seeing the otherwise cheerful man sad.

"Gwen."

Jason looked confused.

"It's my name," I said, and it was surprisingly hard to say.

He grinned again, and this time his smile was infectious. "Nice to meet you Gwen."

Jasper came over and lay down at my feet. I absently ran my hand through his soft fur and tried not to notice the awkward silence.

"So what did you do, you know, before?" I asked.

"Before the apocalypse?"

I nodded.

"I was at Princeton, studying criminal justice."

"You were going to be a lawyer?"

"Yep," he said, "It sort of runs in my family. Everyone is either a lawyer, a cop or in the Marines. Were," he corrected sadly, "They were."

I reached out from under my blankets and took his hand. It was warm and calloused, but when he squeezed it back I knew I had made the right call.

"My little sister, she wanted to be a vet. She loved animals."

"I'm sorry." I didn't know what else to say.

Jason looked at me, "It's ok. I guess we've all lost someone we love. Tell me about your family."

I looked at the ground, "It was just me and my dad. My mum died when I was three. My dad was the owner of all these big companies, I didn't really know what they were though. We were rich and I was spoilt. They used to call my dad the 'King of Business' because he did so well." I swallowed, thinking about my dad was making me tear up. "He always used to joke that if he was the king then I was his princess."

I couldn't see past the tears silently streaming down my face. Jason put a warm arm around me and I leaned into the one armed hug, grateful that just for one night, I wasn't alone.

oooooo

The next morning, I awoke feeling better rested than I had in weeks. My back was really warm, and I turned over to find Jason lying against me, still asleep. Blushing, I quickly sat up and pretended to be searching through my pack whilst I got my emotions under control. I wasn't sure what I felt for Jason, he was sweet, funny, handsome, but there was still this air of mystery about him. My heart wanted me to go for it, my gut told me to be careful.

Jason found me later in the house, using a portable gas cooker I had found in the pantry to cook some breakfast.

"That smells good," he said, sleepily rubbing his eyes. Jasper bounded in after him and gave me the saddest puppy dog eyes.

I rolled my eyes, "Fine," I said and gave him a sliver of the canned meat I was cooking up.

"You've just made a friend for life," Jason said, over his own meal.

I laughed a short, sharp sound that made me pause. I couldn't remember the last time I had laughed. But it felt good to do so, like a balloon lifting a weight off my chest.

"So what are your plans?" Jason asked.

"I'm not sure yet," I replied. "I just know I need to get out of town."

"Why are the DRAGONS after you anyway? I've never seen so many in pursuit of one person."

I used the pretence of cleaning up as a reason not to look Jason in the eye. "I don't know," I said, shrugging.

I felt strong fingers on my chin, pulling my gaze up into the vibrant green of Jason's eyes. "You can trust me," he said, smiling gently.

My eyes lingered on Jason's full lips and I wondered what it would feel like to kiss them.

"Gwen," he said.

I looked up, and then found out exactly what it was like to kiss those lips because they were suddenly and almost ferociously on mine. His arms went around my body, pulling me into his own and I was surrounded by Jason's warm, masculine scent. I kissed him back with just as much passion, with lips that had not been kissed this way before. Jason's kiss made me realise that in comparison everything I had ever thought of as a kiss was just a substitute for the real thing. We both had to pull away, practically gasping for air, and my body already mourned the loss of his warmth.

"I...I... what was that?"

Jason grinned, stroking a finger over my cheek, "Haven't you ever been kissed before?"

"Not like that." My fingers fluttered over my lips.

Jason's fingers grazed over my scar and his face tightened as if he felt my pain, "How did this happen?"

I pulled away. "It's nothing."

Jason grabbed my arm and gently brought me back. "It's not nothing. Tell me."

"I got in a fight, ok? I needed some food more than the other guy did and I paid for it."

I didn't want to tell Jason that Lucas had done that to me. When he began his world domination and his robots were taking over, he had held me at knife point in front of my father. My father pleaded with him to let me go, but the lunatic just laughed and scarred me forever. He said that now he was the only one who would want me. And then he threw the knife at my father where it embedded in his chest. He died, bloody and gasping in my arms.

Jason frowned at my response, perhaps detecting the lie in my voice, but he let it go.

"We should probably get going, we're losing daylight."

He nodded in agreement and we both headed back to the barn to pack up our gear.

oooooo

It was nice to have a travelling companion. It's a bit hard to play *I spy* by yourself. I enjoyed watching Jasper exploring the countryside as we walked mile after mile down the highway. The rusted shells of cars where everywhere, and we saw rotting piles of bodies lined up along the street. In the city, most had been burned or buried already, but out here there was no one to do it, so they were left to the birds.

As we walked, Jason and I exchanged stories, and it was such a pleasant comparison to how I normally spent the time, stressing about Lucas and his robots. With each hour, Jason seemed more and more worried, and our conversation dwindled until all that could be heard was the light tread of our footsteps. I wondered what was on his mind, but assumed he was thinking about the same things I was.

The sun was just beginning to lower over the horizon when Jason stopped in the middle of the road. I had been searching the sides, looking for somewhere we might be able to camp out for the night, and didn't notice his sudden lack of movement straight away. When I did, I turned back to him. "Everything alright?"

Jason shook his head. "I can't. I'm sorry." His usual cheerful demeanour was gone and he seemed pale.

I frowned, "You can't what? What's wrong?"

"I just... I'm sorry Gwen. He has her. Chloe. My sister."

It took a moment for his words to sink in before I realised who he was talking about. I gasped, "Lucas?" I started backing away from Jason, my expression slowly turning from confused to horrified.

"I'm sorry," he repeated, pulling a hand gun out of the waistband of his jeans. "I don't have a choice. I don't want to do this."

"There's always a choice," I shouted, "Please."

Jason closed his eyes for a moment and took a deep breath, I saw his shoulders harden in resolve and that's when I turned and ran.

My heart was pounding and my feet slapped the ground, but Jason was faster. He grabbed my arm and pulled me around to him. I flailed at him with my free arm and tried to kick him in the shin, but he was stronger. Over his shoulder, I saw the tell-tale red beams of DRAGONS scanners approaching in the distance and renewed my struggles.

"Let me go!" I screamed, but Jason held on tighter. I managed to nail him in the eye with my fist but he just grunted, absorbing the blow.

"I'm sorry!" he said, before cold-cocking me in the temple with his gun.

oooooo

Feeling like I was waking up with a hang over after a hard night of partying, I rolled over and peeled my eyes open. Thank God the lights were dimmed. Putting a hand to my head, I massaged my temples but was confused to find a small bump over my right eye. In a flood, my last memories came rushing back to me and I gasped and jumped up from the bed I was lying on. I immediately regretted it, as I had to lean over on the bed for support, until my shaky legs could take my weight.

"That bastard," I said, thinking of Jason. But the words didn't really feel right in my mouth, as if deep down, I didn't really believe them. I thought of the look in his eyes as he told me about his sister. I didn't envy him right now.

The door to the small room opened and Lucas strode in. As usual, his black hair was in disarray and judging from the stubble on his jaw, it had been a while since he'd last shaved. He towered over me, with a smirk that told said he had finally won.

"Gwenevere, my queen. At last you have been returned to me."

"I see you're still delusional Lucas," I retorted.

He invaded my personal space, forcing me to back up a few steps. "Now, now. Is that any way to treat your husband and king?"

"You are not my king and you are definitely not my husband!" I sneered, fury overwhelming my mind.

Quicker than a whip, Lucas backhanded me, sending me reeling back onto the bed. Combined with the lump on my forehead, my brain was getting quite sore.

I spat blood out of my mouth, and looked him straight in the eyes. "I will die before I become your queen."

"That can be arranged my dear. But let's see how amenable you are after a spell in the dungeons. Knight!" He called out.

"Really?" I said, "You have knights? Who would agree to be part of your insanity?"

"Not knights," he said, smirking, "KNIGHT. My **K**ing's **N**ew **I**ndestructible **G**ruesome **H**ardworking **T**echno."

My eyes widened as what looked to be a suit of armour walked into the room. It was completely black and walked with a loud clanking. I scooted back, but the KNIGHT leaned down and painfully grabbed my arm and hauled me out of the room. I tried to wrench free, but it was completely metal and incredibly solid. Lucas' manic laughter followed me out into the hallway. The KNIGHT wordlessly marched me down flight after flight of stairs and practically threw me into a modified jail cell, slamming the door shut behind me. It then turned and stood guard in front of the door. It was as still as a statue and I was afraid to even breathe in its direction.

I looked around my jail cell, but apart from a cot and a toilet, it was bare. I slumped down on the bed, wondering how I would get myself out of this situation.

"Hey!" A voice whispered from behind me. I turned around to see a girl of no more than twelve or thirteen sitting in a cell identical to mine, but three cells down. She had long chestnut brown hair and looked as though she had been here for a while.

"Who are you?" she asked.

"I'm Gwen."

"Chloe."

I gasped. "You're Jason's sister, aren't you?"

The girl smiled with relief. "Yes. How do you know him? Is he ok?"

"He's fine," I said, swallowing a lump in my throat, "He turned me into Lucas for you."

Chloe gasped. "Why would he do that? He's such an idiot." She lowered her voice. "I totally have an escape plan lined up."

My eyes widened in disbelief. "Really? What is it?"

Chloe looked sheepish. "Well, um... it involves a lot of lock picking and a few distractions..."

"You don't really have an escape plan, do you?"

She looked at her feet, "No. At least not one that will work."

I sighed and flopped down onto my cot. "Great."

I wasn't sure how long I had been lying there when the gate at the entrance to the cells squealed open and I sat up to see who was there. I recognised Jason's shaggy hair and green eyes and my heart fluttered before I remembered what he did to me. I narrowed my eyes at him and sent him what I hoped was a telepathic message that involved him doing something anatomically impossible.

Jason walked straight past me, not making eye contact, and went straight to his sister's cell.

"Jason!" cried Chloe.

"Are you alright?" he asked "Did he hurt you?"

"I'm fine, you moron," said Chloe, and Jason looked surprised. "How could you let them take Gwen?"

Jason rubbed the back of his neck. "I had to. There was no other choice."

Chloe crossed her arms and stared at him. "You are such an idiot."

"Yeah, yeah, I know," Jason mumbled under his breath.

The KNIGHT walked to Chloe's cell and unlocked it, allowing her to leave. As the two hugged and then walked past me, Jason stopped. His eyes bore into mine, trying to convey something I couldn't understand.

"Gwen, please forgive me. I didn't want to betray you."

I wanted so badly to hurt him in the same way he hurt me, but I just couldn't do it. "It's ok, I understand. I would have done the same."

Jason didn't look relieved, but he reached through the bars and clasped my hands. "I could make a thousand apologies and it still wouldn't be enough." I felt something rectangular and metal in my hands, and quickly slipped it into my pocket out of sight of the KNIGHT.

Jason looked into my eyes and subtly winked at me, before wrapping his arm around Chloe and leaving the cell.

I stared down at the device in my hand; it was the low frequency disrupter Malcolm had made for me. I don't know how long it would last for, or even how well it would work but Jason had given me a chance.

The next day, the KNIGHT removed me from my cell and marched me back up into the building. I was dragged before Lucas who was sitting on a throne made of metal. He had a crown filled with electrical wires and jewels perched lopsided atop his head which just made him look ridiculous.

Around him little robots polished the floor and cleaned the room. At my questioning glance he said, "Do you like my newest invention? They are SERFS or **S**mall **E**motionless **R**obots **F**or **S**ervitude." His eyes gleamed with pride.

"What do you want?" I asked.

"Gwenevere. You will be my queen soon. You must start acting the part."

"Never," I hissed at him, hatred in my eyes.

He walked down to me, and cupped my chin in his hand. Even though it was the same gesture Jason had done what seemed like forever ago in that farm kitchen, it felt cold and distant in comparison. I yanked my face out of his grasp and glared at him.

He grabbed my face again and traced the scar running along my face. "I remember this. What an ugly scar. No one else will find you beautiful now."

Even as he said the words, my mind went to Jason and I knew that someone did find me beautiful.

"I also remember throwing my knife into your father and watching you weep pathetically over his cold dead body."

His cruel words had the intended effect, my rage boiled up and I lunged at him, hoping to scrape out his eyeballs with my fingernails. Before I could get close enough, the KNIGHT grabbed me and pinned my arms against my sides.

"I hate you!" I spit out.

Even though the KNIGHT was pinning my arms to my sides, I was still able to reach into my pocket and press the button on the low frequency disrupter. The KNIGHT went still, arms hanging by its sides as if it had suddenly decided to turn itself off. The SERFS did the same, pausing in whatever task they were doing.

Lucas looked at his robots in a panic. "What have you done?" he screamed.

I grinned slowly at him. "I evened the playing field, you lunatic."

I removed the sword from the KNIGHT's scabbard; it came out with a hiss. Although it was a little heavy, I'm no longer the lightweight I used to be. Lucas backed away from me, true fear in his face. "No please!" he said, holding his arms out in front of him.

"This is for my father," I said and thrust the sword deep into his chest.

He stared down in disbelief at the weapon protruding from his body. His eyes rolled into the back of his head, and he fell forward onto the ground.

I left that bastard's body where it lay and left his lair, knowing what I had to do. I made sure that the DRAGONS would never come after anyone again.

I emerged outside to find I had been inside a modern building designed to look like a castle. What was with that guy and all his medieval references?

Jason and Chloe were waiting for me outside. I stopped when I saw them, unsure if Jason would try to stop me.

"I was stupid," He started.

"I know."

He grinned.

"Come on," I said.

"Will they still come after us?" Chloe asked, obviously meaning the robots. She looked toward the castle with a twinkle of fear in her eyes.

I shook my head, "No, I found the main control panel for all of Lucas' machines and destroyed it. Besides, machines are only as capable as the person that's controlling them, and well... that person is dead."

Jason grabbed my hand. "Can I ever apologise enough?"

"No," I replied, "but kissing me might make it better."

He grinned as he leaned toward me to comply.

ABOUT SARA OPALKA

Sara Opalka lives in Adelaide, South Australia. She has recently completed a Bachelor of Arts at the University of Adelaide with a major in English and minors in Classics and Creative Writing. She is obsessed with time travel, procrastinating and what her survival action plan would be if the world ended. If she had a superpower, it would be the ability to stop time so she could slap people who annoy her. *Beware: Here be DRAGONS* is her first published work.

The Door Mouse Does Death A Favor

by Windsor Potts

The Door Mouse did not like to be disturbed when he was bathing. It suited his temper to take his time to lather up, scrub, rinse, towel off, and then powder himself. During this particular bath, someone rang the buzzer at the front door, and the Door Mouse muttered as he dripped down the hallway. "Oh, I'll never get the blood out of my fur at this rate." He opened the latch, water still running down his snout, and gruffly asked, "Yes, yes, what do you want?"

With a scythe leaned over his shoulder, Death towered above the Door Mouse's childlike frame. He was twice the size of a full grown man, draped in a heavy, dingy, sun-faded grey hood and cloak. "Greetings, Mouse. I seem to have gotten you at a bad time. I do apologize."

Wiping drops of water from his whiskers, the Door Mouse waved off the apology. "Not to worry, Sir. I'm sure you catch people at more awkward times. It has been a while since I've seen you. How may I be of service to you, Sir?" When Death didn't reply, the Door Mouse remembered his manners. "I'm sorry, Sir, won't you come in?"

Death followed the wet trail that the Door Mouse left into the kitchen. Death pulled out a chair, propped his scythe against a wall, and leaning back, placed his hands on his knees. The Door Mouse used a blue gingham kitchen towel to wipe his snout dry. "If I may ask, Sir, is it now my appointed final time to meet with you?" Holding the towel over the sink, the mouse squeezed it dry, wringing out a bloody, soapy mixture, and lay it on the counter.

The grey cowl shook from side to side. "No, now is not your time. In fact, it is someone else's time and that's what I came to see you about. I noticed the bit of work you did just before your bath and I want your help in this matter."

Pulling out his own chair, the Door Mouse climbed into it, and stood across from Death, twitching his whiskers in a rather pleased manner. "Well, Sir, I must say I'm flattered you noticed. This village was a bit of work, but I got it all done in a day, as is my habit."

With a skeletal finger pointing towards the door they had entered, Death replied, "This village is a military instillation. You killed an entire army. Flattery in this case would fall short of its true mark."

Shrugging, the Door Mouse laced his lithe fingers together, and placed them on his fat belly as he leaned against the back of the chair. "They weren't much of a fight. There were just so many of them. The ones in this little hideaway were the difficult ones."

The bone hand motioned to the structure they sat in. "This little hideaway was their last line of defense. Supposedly, they build these to prevent things like you from happening to the people inside them."

Tapping a knowing fur-covered claw next to his snout, the Door Mouse winked and replied, "But getting into places is what I'm good at, Sir. And killing the stuff there..." He looked at the bodies of the soldiers that littered the floor and the smiled at Death. "Well, Sir, that's just a privilege."

The cowl nodded as Death rested his hands upon his knees again. "That is the level of skill I need. Also, the creatures of your original realm are not known for dying easily, which will benefit you for where I am to send you."

Leaning onto the table, the Door Mouse propped his head upon his hands. "Really now? And where exactly is that?"

oooooo

Moving through the Tunnels always made the Door Mouse hungry. He kept a portion of dried meat in a small satchel, right beside a flask of cold tea and a very, very sharp knife. The Tunnels compressed gravity and magnetism into another force of attraction, one so strong that it not only distorted time and space, but also the Planes of Existence and Possibility. This attraction didn't penetrate every single dimension, but it had the ability to do so, if it so chose.

That was the secret of how the Door Mouse was able to move anywhere he liked: He was made of the stuff of the Tunnels. His birth world existed on a plane that the Tunnels all led to and the reality there was very silly indeed. Nothing was serious. Even the threat of killing someone held no weight, because no one ever

129

really died. That's why the Door Mouse left years ago. He grew bored of nothing ever dying. And deep down, he knew he was made to kill.

He'd detected his victim's scent, and moved into the Tunnel, nibbling on some dried meat. As he floated down the length of the shaft, pictures danced by his eyes. Some of them were ghosts, some of them were memories from previous lives, and some of them were phantoms of a different realm. It was a place of pain, torment, and suffering, and he did not care for those things. As his feet reached the tunnel's end, he mumbled, "It's not natural to torture something so."

He came to a very large door with some indecipherable writing above it. He walked to the door, and went to move through, but it resisted. The Door Mouse bumped his snout and grumbled, "Well, well, what a cup of tea this is." He pulled the flask of cold tea out of his satchel and knocked on the great door before him.

Soon the lock rattled, the hinges squealed, and a Cyclops gird in a black loincloth peered around the door's edge. "What do you want?"

"How come I can't get through the door?"

Squinting with his one great eye, the Cyclops stared at the Door Mouse and then at the great door he held open. "My Lord had this door bought from a land far away, made so that only those like us could come in. Once again, what do you want, little mouse?"

Looking over the Cyclops's head, the Door Mouse pointed to the door post with his free hand as he placed the flask of cold tea into his satchel. "Your sign is misspelled."

Stepping out, the Cyclops read the sign quietly, and then turned to face the Door Mouse. "No it isn't. It clearly says, 'Abandon h-'." His words were cut off by the gurgling sound that came out of his throat as the very, very sharp knife passed through it. The Door Mouse wiped the blood on the Cyclops's body as he walked through the doorway, and into the bowels of Hell. He was going to kill the Devil, one way or another.

oooooo

As the Door Mouse walked through the circles of Hell, the more irritated he became. He grumbled and mumbled as he descended deeper into the pits. "I can't stand all these screams. Something needs to be done." After continuing on for several more miles, he saw a group of small demons, jumping around a pit, tormenting the hapless souls below, attacking them with spears and whips.

The Door Mouse twitched his whiskers briskly, and then calmed himself by stroking them before approaching one of the

130

demons and asking, "Excuse me? What would a soul have to do to get the attention of the Devil himself?"

The diminutive demon stood eye to eye with the Door Mouse, and then used the handle of his whip to scratch his chin as he thought. "Well, it would probably have to be a soul so obstinate and unrepentant that even one of the Lords of the Realm couldn't handle it."

Nodding, the Door Mouse pulled gently at the end of his whiskers. "I see. You're not one of these Lords of the Realm, by chance, are you?"

After a surprised laugh, the demon replied, "What? Oh my, but no. I'm but an Imp. Not even a Squire. Above them are the Knights, the Masters, the Gallions, Bastions, Ephemerals, the Vices, and then the Lords."

Pulling the very, very sharp knife out of the satchel, the Door Mouse sighed. "I had a feeling it would be something like that." With a simple swipe, he beheaded the Imp before him and then waded into the heavily armed crowd before him.

oooooo

As a second Lord of the Realm lay dead at the Door Mouse's feet, another one fled from before him. It half-run and half-flew, his bat-like wings not able to get clearance above the mounds of demonic bodies that surrounded the Door Mouse.

Within moments, Lucifer appeared, dressed in a white robe, his hair long and dark, with beautiful white wings on his back. His face was handsome and confused. "I'm not sure who you are or why you are here, but I'm afraid you've made a grave mistake."

Pointing his very, very sharp knife at the Devil, the Door Mouse addressed him in a less than respectful manner. "I am the Door Mouse and I've come to end you. And the sooner, the better. I've grown bored and disgusted with your realm."

A besmirched look crossed the Devil's face. "So, you're the Door Mouse. I've wanted you down here for some while now. In fact, it seems not long ago that I made a wager with my friend Death that he could not claim you and deliver you into my kingdom."

The voice of Death sounded from behind the Door Mouse. "A wager that I have delivered on. Now, friend Lucifer, I would like my bride."

The Door Mouse turned his gaze between Lucifer and Death. His look wasn't one of pain or confusion, but one who sought the truth. "Sir? You sold me out? For some succubus?"

Chiding the Door Mouse, Lucifer explained. "She's far from a succubus. Not really a member of my realm at all. She's an

131

immortal whom has had the misfortune to be trapped here for some time. Death expressed an interest in me finding him a partner that could stand the test of time, so to speak. And here she comes." A creature in a shimmering gown was brought forward, surrounded by a group of demonic denizens. The figure was definitely female, but the face had no discernible feature, not an eye, nose, or mouth. "She is akin to you in nature, born on one of the planes of the gods."

The boney hand of Death reached towards her as he said, "We exchanged one servant for another. And I'll have her now."

The faceless figure recoiled from Death's grip and images appeared above her head, her thoughts becoming moving pictures of her fear of her suitor. A clawed hand of a demon shoved her forward, pushing her to the ground. She fell at the feet of the Door Mouse, and as he stepped to her side, he extended his small paw.

As she got to her knees, he whispered to her, "You really don't want to go with him, do you?" The formless face showed no expression, but tiny images formed above her head. They were so small that only the Door Mouse in front of her could see them, and they kept showing her running away from Death. Looking around at the demons surrounding them, he whispered, "I doubt you want to stay here either." The picture show in front of his eyes was a series of tortures being performed on her, her blank face somehow still managing to show pain. Nodding, the Door Mouse said, "I thought as much. What happens to you when you do die? Your folks have a happy hunting ground or something?"

The images that appeared above her were so large and vivid that they superimposed themselves over the surrounding misery and darkness that was Hell. Instead of cavern walls and looming shadows, the Door Mouse was now surrounded by an Orchard with trees that bloomed not only both fruit and flowers, but leaves that changed colors as the light hit them. The wind whistled beautiful melodies as it wound through branches. There were scents that stirred deep emotions in him, deep even into his past lives, and it caused him to shutter. Then the images disappeared.

He closed his eyes as a tear ran down his snout.

The infernal spectators that surrounded them had been ignorant to the first images but the encompassing vision of the Orchard hit them like a wall of flame. The Devil barked angrily, "What's going on here?"

With unmatched speed, the Door Mouse had his very, very sharp knife at the throat of the faceless woman. "We're renegotiating your bargain. It seems neither she or I are satisfied with being your pawns."

The Devil snarled. "You are a fool, Mouse. Death closed the

door entered, so you can not escape my kingdom. The woman is an immortal, much like you, and your paltry blade can not harm her, so give Death his prize. Furthermore, for all that you've done, I'm going to make your eternity here most unpleasant, I promise you."

Twitching his whiskers, the Door Mouse said, "You're wrong on two accounts. Firstly, this is no paltry blade; it's a very, very sharp knife. From my home world. And thought she is immortal, much like me, she is not from my world." With that, he leans forward and whispers towards the empty face, "I am, for the first time in my life, sorry for what I'm about to do." He pulled the very, very sharp knife across her throat and then sank it into her chest.

There was no blood. There was nothing but a great silence throughout all of Hell. Even as the Devil and Death screamed, their words were absorbed into the void of soundlessness that rang throughout the realm. Then light exploded from the woman's body and flakes, like a thousand mirrored snowflakes, floated down. "The other thing you didn't take into account is that I only use a door to enter. I don't need one to leave." And without another word, he disappeared.

oooooo

In the annals of Time and Space, it is said that Death and the Devil never spoke again. Death reportedly scoured all of the realities he could to find the Door Mouse, all to no avail. The Devil sat in his kingdom, sulking for a century as he rebuilt the army the Door Mouse destroyed in less than a day.

The Door Mouse returned home, to his original plane, as much as it pained him to do so. He sat at a table set with many places, yet he only had two companions. Both were lunatics, but they were fairly powerful and good company to him. They drank tea while the Door Mouse regularly dosed himself with a potion that wiped his memory out for lengthy periods of time. The potion made him sleep and he would dream of the Tunnels, women made of stars, the sound his knife made as he sank it into living flesh, and long, hot baths.

Sometimes though, the potion would wear off, and he would remember. He could still see the trees in the Orchard, the colors of the leaves, and hear the sweetest music playing as the breeze moved through the branches. And he never wanted to remember that again.

133

About Windsor Potts

Windsor Potts is an alchemist, philosopher, minister, and poet. He has a collection of short stories and sayings set to release in 2014, entitled *Bones in the Playground, Children at the Grave.* He engages in general debauchery and hedonism, mostly in the form of smoking cigars. You can find him on Facebook as the writer, Windsor Potts.

Wolves At The Door

by Andrea L. Staum

The girl stared up at the forty story high metal wall that surrounded Fortress and gave the city its name. No one remembered how thick it was and no one had seen beyond it for several generations. Not even grandmother, the oldest person she knew, could say for sure what lay beyond the structure. Even as she pressed with questions, she was repeatedly told there was nothing beyond the wall.

"Where do the images come from?" she asked.

Grandmother stopped a few strides away from her and turned. "Now what are you going on about?"

"In class, they bring up pictures of what it used to be like before the wall. Where did they get those images?"

"Databases," replied the old woman curtly. "Now, hurry."

The girl continued staring at the wall. Maintenance crews had been through recently and a fresh coat of copper sealant had been applied. The lights from the nearest building reflected back, casting a soft glow over the walkway.

She reached out to touch the wall. "Where did the databases get them from?"

Grandmother gave an exacerbated sigh; grabbing the girl's arm she led her away. "Someone was thoughtful enough to upload them long ago."

"Are you sure? Couldn't they be of what's really out there?"

Grandmother shook her head. "Of course I'm sure. There is nothing beyond the wall."

Even with the old woman's hurried steps, she couldn't keep from watching the seamless wall. There were no weld marks along in. She hadn't been allowed to walk the complete circumference because her clearance level would not allow her in some sectors, but somehow she knew there had to be a way to see if there was something out there or not.

"Juliet! You'll be late for class," Grandmother scolded as they turned into the tunnel that housed the imagers. "What are they teaching today?"

Juliet shrugged. She had skipped the past few class hours and Grandmother knew it. She had found more interesting simulations in the database and spent the time exploring them instead of the boring classes the Educators insisted were needed. That was why the old woman insisted on taking her to the imagers, to make sure she loaded the correct program. A thought crept into her mind. "Grandmother?" she asked tentatively, knowing the woman was losing patience and was making herself late for her shift at the hospital.

"What?"

"If there's nothing beyond the wall, where are my classmates from?" she asked.

Grandmother rolled her dark eyes. "Fortress."

They had reached the imager bank. Several other students were strapping the image glasses on and making sure the sanitation packs were secured. Biting her lip, the girl pressed on, "But I've been all over and there are still nearly thirty people I've never seen."

"Different rotations," Grandmother replied as she lifted the shield off an imager and began preparing it for her.

"If they're different rotations, wouldn't they be in different classes?"

Grandmother shook her head. "Enough of your talk, plug yourself in." Grandmother keyed in her ID. "Looks like they have you making up your time. Best put a pack on and a diet stream too. I won't be seeing you for nearly two days."

The girl grimaced but took a tube out of her shoulder pocket, hooking it to the supplement machine before stepping into the imager. "Are you sure I can't help you at the hospital?"

Grandmother pushed her down into the seat and started forcing the tube down her throat. "Stop it. If you don't do the classes you might get your wish and find out what's beyond the wall. No need for laziness in Fortress. If you can't contribute, what's the point of you?"

The girl pouted and let the girdle belt wrap around her middle and connected the sanitation pack. She slid the glasses into place and reached for the keypad, but Grandmother batted her hand away.

"I don't trust you," the old woman said and entered the lesson code, pulling the jack cord out of the socket once the machine released it. She keyed an alarm on her wrist brace. "I'll be back when this goes off. Now plug yourself in."

The girl took the cord from her grandmother's hand and plugged it into her temple jack. The image was slow in coming, but she was in one of the older imagers. She closed her eyes and when she opened them, Grandmother was gone and she was in the standard white-walled classroom, lined with boring white desks and no semblance of reality.

"She keyed the wrong program," the girl grumbled when she looked around. The last lesson she had attended was a science based program, she should be in a lab setting, not this sterile cell. There were several other students with her, but they were not her classmates. In fact she did not recognize anyone except the preloaded instructor, Unit 6, an androgynous being that had been coded to have all the pleasing features that would nurture young minds.

"Juliet Donavan," stated Unit 6 when she finished the boot up process. Usually the voice of the instructor was one of the Educators, this one was set to the melodic default. "You have missed three credits worth of material and must relaunch where you left off. Fortunately, another rotation is on the same schedule as you are and authorization has been granted for you to join them. Upon leaving the program it is advised that you thank the Educators for this opportunity."

Juliet smiled sweetly at the digital personification of the Educators. "Of course, Unit 6."

Unit 6 inclined its head. "Those in this rotation have been selected for Defense and Surveying. You have been recoded and will be joining them from now on. This is an accelerated rotation."

"Now hold on! I'm Botany and Agriculture!" objected Juliet.

Unit 6 tilted its head to the side while it processed the information and downloaded orders from the Educators. When it spoke again, Juliet shuddered as the gruff voice of Educator Mahigan came out of its genderless face. "Your lack of dedication has forced the Educators to reassign you. Your scores in the physical performance and your inquisitiveness in regards to what is beyond the wall, has proven you better suited for this task."

"I know nothing of Defense!"

Unit 6 returned to its melodic voice. "Irrelevant. The decision has been made. A formal complaint can be filed upon completion of the rotation."

"Completion?"

"Yes, there will be no daily breaks in this rotation. The student will remain within the image ducts for the duration. Your family has been notified of the change. Now please take your seat, we have lost time." Unit 6 turned away from her and made its way to the front of the room.

Juliet looked around. She was the only one still standing; the rest of the students had taken their seats. Most did not acknowledge her, keeping the blank expression often seen on those who wore the mark of De/Su. There were a few bewildered expressions on those who kept looking at their signature stripes in confusion. There was only one person Juliet recognized and that girl did not looked pleased with the program either as she plucked at the stripes on her arm

She looked down at her own uniform and saw that her blue Bo/Ag stripes had been rewritten to the green and brown. Before she slumped into her chair she noticed one boy staring at her. He inclined his head at her before turning his attention back to Unit 6.

"You are all high level tested individuals," Unit 6 started when she finally took her seat. This time the voice was one Juliet did not recognize. Then again, she had only taken one defense class at the insistence of her father. "That is why you have been selected. Some of you are not familiar with Defense and Surveying and even if you are De/Su, you do not know me." Unit 6 glitched and was replaced with a tall uniformed man. Unlike most instructors, he claimed a faulted image with a scar running across his cheek, it was never easy to tell if he had coded himself that way to appear more menacing, or didn't know how to code a perfected image. "I am Commander Vilks of Fortress." An audible breath could be heard from several of the stone-faced students and Vilks allowed a half smile the other half unable to come due to the scar. "I see that some of you do know the name."

"Sir," a broad shouldered boy in the front of the room stood. "I don't recognize you, but I know Fortress and I can tell you, it doesn't exist."

"What?!" gasped the girl Juliet had recognized. "Are you daft? Or do they not tell you where you are when they take you to the barracks as babes?"

"Don't know what you're talking about Miss, I'm jacked in on Independence, part of Uchdryd," the soldier replied.

"Uchdryd? What is that? Some sewer level? Have you been so long down below you have forgot what the sun is?" asked the girl.

The boy straightened. "Uchdryd is the floating city. Burditt and I are jacked in on the main barge, Independence." He turned to the boy who had nodded at Juliet. "Do you recognize any of them, Burditt?"

The other boy shrugged. "No, Sergeant, but I think if you

sit down and let Commander Vilks speak, we may get to know a hell of a lot more about what's going on.

The commander nodded. "There are fourteen sanctuaries throughout the world and all think they are the only one. Only a select few now this and now you can count yourself among them."

"Preposterous!" The girl shouted. "The records state there are no survivors outside the wall."

The commander sat on the corner of the instructor's desk. "Faith Seher, I presume?"

She nodded.

Vilks folded his arms across his chest. "I hate to tell you this, Faith, but the Historical database isn't all encompassing. Some files are held back for the safety of the populace, but you know that. After all, you weren't chosen for your Library/History stripes."

She scoffed.

"Each of you was selected for different reasons, but all of you have expressed interest in what may be beyond your homes," Vilks straightened and turned to the wall behind him. A map loaded and fourteen points were marked on it. Most of them were stationary, but two of them moved, one slightly, the other erratically. "There are fourteen Sanctuaries throughout the world and all of them think they are the last one. Only a select few know the truth, not even all the Educators know what I am about to tell you. This is the first time that the De/Su units from each location are working together and the top minds of the Sanctuaries have been chosen to help us."

Juliet snorted through her nose.

The commander turned to her. "Yes?"

"Top minds? You expect me to believe I was chosen for top marks? Even I'll admit I'm a slacker."

"You were chosen for your general curiosity. Your grandmother filed a report on your tendency toward distraction and we feel that ability to look beyond what is presented will be an asset in what we are about to face."

"And what is that?" the sergeant asked.

Vilks gestured to the map and three lights blinked out. "These Sanctuaries recently went off the grid and two others have reported troubles." Two of the lights began flashing. "They are finding breaches in their containment zones and gaps in their program data. Something from the outside is trying to get in."

Faith shook her head vehemently, causing a few strands of her golden curls to fall lose from their pins. "There's nothing beyond the wall!"

"Oh, Ms. Seher, there is. There are wolves at our door and

you few selected are going to help keep them at bay, if not eradicate them," replied the commander as he clapped his hands together, the program allowed the sound to echo through the room and the light glitched.

Juliet found herself in another room with Faith, Burditt and two others. It was an infinity lab often used in the programing classes or science. Several stations were blocked off from view by codewalls, but could easily be accessed with the proper codes. The map shone down with them; now three lights were flashing above them. She looked to the other four. "What happened?"

Vilks appeared with an instructor Unit 6 who explained, "The class has been divided into work groups. This is yours."

"The lights. Why are three flashing?" one of the boys Juliet couldn't identify inquired.

"A new attack has begun. You must hurry. What information we have is in the consoles. Faith of Fortress and Matiu of Descent will be able to bypass any security issues you may encounter. Their hacking skills are the reason they are here after all."

The boy who had not spoken had already booted up the console and was busy at the controls. Faith joined him.

"What is our purpose?" asked the first boy.

"Delsin of Tower, you know what is allowed by the rules of the Sanctuaries. I look to you to keep everything ethical. Burditt of Uchdryd, you have a military way of thinking and will know proper procedure," explained the instructor image.

Vilks cleared his throat. "The 6 will be here to answer any questions you may have. It will also be in contact with the De/Su Commanders. If you have any concerns present them to the Unit," he replied before blinking out of the program.

They gathered around the console as Faith pulled up the information about the attacks. Images flashed across the walls. More lights began to flash on the map above them as they read through file after file.

"The threat is organic," Matiu said at length, leaning back in his chair. "Humanoid even, but clearly not of higher intelligence or they would have hacked all the systems quicker. The attack on the first Sanctuary took longer than the rest."

"I just don't understand why." grumbled Faith.

"Location," replied Juliet. "The first attack was in a more open than the rest."

Burditt shook his head. "That doesn't make sense. The Sanctuaries are inaccessible from outside threat. Fortress with its wall, Uchdryd by water, Tower rises sheer from the ground while Descent is underground."

"An asset when attacked from outside, but a weakness from within," continued Juliet. "Which means things can infiltrate and eat away at the populace easily. With the open concept the first Sanctuary, the people could spread out and make it harder to attack."

"We have it!" Delsin exclaimed. "The wolves aren't at the door, they're already through it."

Juliet rocked back on her heels, pondering the possibilities.

"If that's the case, how can we find them?" asked Matiu.

Unit 6 tilted its head. "Tower is under attack. Delsin, you are being called out of the program."

Delsin jerked and stared up at the map. Two of the flashing lights had blinked out and a new one had begun.

Burditt frowned. "We'll keep working here while you log out and attend to things at Tower."

Dalsin wrung his hands. "We seemed to be onto something," he muttered before disappearing.

"Well then," Matiu said, "time to dig deeper. I can send Tower a message when we figure something out. Juliet, can you see if there's something we can do for Delsin?"

Juliet nodded and started reviewing the inventory of Tower to see what they might have that could be converted into a biological aerosol to use against an internal foe without hurting the general population. The cliff dwelling Sanctuary had an impressive stock and she began comparing it with her Botany curriculum.

Faith smiled. "I'll start running them ragged." And the blonde began tapping away at the console in front of her.

Unit 6 stared blankly ahead, but tilted its head indicating an incoming message. "The group has started into the loophole mechanics," it stated before the room flickered.

The four of them found themselves in a new simulation. Unit 6 was no longer with them and the infinity lab was gone. They were in a dark, stone room with a single console rising from the center of the room. The map still shone down on them, the flashing lights of the attacked Sanctuaries giving the only light source. No light came from the console.

Matiu stepped forward and pressed the on button of the screen, as it flared to life three doors illuminated on the wall farthest from them. A keypad was beside each and a pictograph sign glowed down on the group.

Burditt turned to Faith and Matiu. "What did you do?"

Faith put her hands up in defense. "I didn't do anything."

"It's their protection software," added Matiu." We need to work it out and hope we can move on. Clearly Unit 6 was programed by our wolves."

"Three doors and four of us," Juliet pointed out.

"One of us becomes a sacrificial lamb," replied Faith. "The portals will only recognize one cyber signature at a time."

Matiu keyed the databases on console. "We still have access from here, but it will be limited until the code is broken. Juliet, can you still work from here?"

She nodded.

"Doesn't matter if she can. She has to go in," stated Faith.

"Why?"

"Look at the doors. The insignias on top are a fortress and a ship and I think the last one is meant to be a tower. Without Dalsin we couldn't access it, but Fortress has to be similar. Your cave will be nothing like it."

"You're guessing," scoffed Burditt.

She nodded. "I am, but I'd be the most likely to figure out the codes with my hacking skills and history stripes."

"You know nothing about Tower."

"I've run circles around Director Atuc breaking into the databases, there's no reason I can't do this," boasted Faith, setting her hands akimbo.

Burditt stepped forward. "Okay, Matiu you'll stay here and monitor what you can." He stepped toward the door marked with the ship.

Faith brushed past him and hit the buttons to open the Tower marked door without a look back. They caught a glimpse of the stock images of a countryside meadow. Faith stepped through and looked over her shoulder at them. "For better or worse," she chimed before the door slid shut.

Matiu fidgeted behind them. "Juliet, be careful. There's going to be two path signatures from Fortress. It might mean that they can trace back to it. I should have gone in instead of Faith."

"She had a point, her Hist/Lib stripes might do her some good," replied Burditt.

"We don't know what's behind the doors."

A scream echoed through the room and the door that Faith had walked through disappeared.

Burditt turned to Juliet. "If you get in trouble, I'll try and find you."

He squared his shoulders and palmed the button. A harsh wind blew through the door as it opened and snow flurries danced across the floor. An animal howl echoed in the chamber, cut short as the door closed behind the boy.

"One challenge at a time, soldier," she whispered to the shut door and pressed the button to open hers.

She stepped into a forest. She knelt and ran her hands over the warm, brown earth. What lay before her was like nothing she had seen outside of simulation. The tech creating the simulation was tightly coded. "Dirt?" she asked, turning to show the others, but the door had changed. She turned her attention back to the forest ahead. With each step she felt tingles against her skin as her simulation began to pixelate and transform. Her back arched and she dropped down to all fours and saw paws in the place of her hands.

She looked up and the forest had changed to grey tones except for a flash of red that made its way through the trees. A growl started low in her throat, catching her by surprise and she began to lope through the trees, keeping back and watching the figure skip down a well worn path.

She knew the story. Grandmother had told it to her when she was little. Somehow the old woman equated it to the dangers of leaving Fortress. If she were to be the wolf, then she would play it right. She veered away from the path and the red cloaked girl. Going farther into the woods, a cottage came into view. It was a stock image, used in every database to show how wonderful life had been before the walls went up.

Juliet wasn't surprised that the woman raking the front yard had the appearance of her grandmother. Clearly, the program was tapped into her own psyche to create the challenge. She sneaked around the house, grabbing a sheet from the clothes line in her mouth as she passed. She forced her canine body onto its hind legs to wrap the sheet around her, trying to cover her floor. The program glitched and she stood in her own form as the sky flashed yellow.

"That's how it's going to be then," she whispered and made her way around the house, wrapping the sheet tighter around herself.

The old woman stopped raking, looking up at Juliet. "Well, dear, I am surprised you have come so far."

"Do you know me?" Juliet asked.

"You are my granddaughter," came the woman's reply and as she set the rake down. "But where are your clothes?"

Juliet's mind raced before settling on a response. "I snagged them on a branch and they unraveled beyond repaired. I borrowed your sheet to cover the rags."

The grandmother figure smiled and gestured to the cottage. "Let us get you something better."

As she stepped over the threshold, Juliet realized the transformation as her vision turned grey again. Before the old woman could react, Juliet turned back and knocked her over.

Placing a large paw against the woman's frail chest, she growled down at her.

"You have come far reacting to the changes," stated the grandmother, the voice shifting into the melody of the Units and shifting into the expressionless image. "You've broken another security level. Now what will you do?" the image asked as it pixalated and disappeared and the room flashed yellow.

Juliet growled again and looked out the doorway. There was a flash of red through monochrome trees. She rushed to the closet and yanked a dressing gown off a hanger. Ducking her head down, Juliet slowly wormed her way into the garment. Folding her ears back she pushed out and shook her body to settle the gown into place and at the end of the shake she had been transformed into human form once more.

"Grandma, what are you doing on your hands and knees?" asked a girl from behind her.

Juliet felt her heart racing as she pushed herself to her feet; clutching for a cap that lay on the floor to pull over her hair. "I dropped something," she replied, keeping her back to the girl.

"Oh my Grandma! How tall you have gotten since I last visited."

"Oh no dearest, you are standing outside and have not taken the step into the house," Juliet replied, bending her knees and slouching her shoulders to appear smaller.

She could hear the girl coming closer. "Oh my Grandma! How black your hair has become since last I visited."

Juliet raised a hand to the cap and tried to tuck her hair more under it. "Oh no dearest, the light is poor in here and I got soot in it from the fire."

"Oh my Grandma!" The girl said as she put a hand on Juliet's shoulder and pulled at her so they faced each other. "How young you have become!"

Juliet rolled her eyes. "I haven't time for this." She forced herself to change back into a wolf and lunged for the girl who screamed and ran from the cottage, dropping the basket she had been carrying.

She fought the urge to chase after the girl and sniffed at the basket. She nudged the blanket away from the contents and lifted a glowing egg in her jaws. The sky flashed yellow once more, startling, forcing her to bite down on the egg.

Juliet gagged. Opening her eyes she was no longer in the program and she reached for her mouth and pulled the diet tube from her throat, choking in the process. The contents were dried and crusted around the edges and nothing came from the supplement bag. The sanitation pack reeked and she ripped it off before stepping out of the booth. On wobbling legs she moved out, leaning against the side of the booth until her strength returned

The lights in the area were dimmed and several of the booths were knocked over, blocking the tunnel. She slid down to the ground and drew her knees to her chest, resting her head against them. The air was heavy and the normally bustling Fortress was silent.

She forced herself to stand and make her way out of the tunnel. She had to climb over an imager and as she got closer she saw a body lying in tunnel mouth. Flies were thick around the body and Juliet brought her shirt collar up over her mouth and nose. She stepped over the corpse, trying not to look down, but the light had reflected on the arm stripes and Juliet knew it was Faith.

A hand grabbed her shoulder causing her to scream until another hand covered her mouth and pulled her back into the tunnel.

"Quiet," she recognized Vilks's voice. "They haven't left."

She turned and faced the commander.

"How long?" she asked.

"They have been here three months."

Juliet's eyes widened. "Three months? The diet stream lasts a week!"

He nodded. "I've been watching it, but ran out. I hoped you would finish before then."

"What about Faith?"

Vilks looked away from her. "Her hacks were drawing attention and I pulled her out. She was discovered and almost brought them back here. She had to be eliminated."

"You killed her?"

He shook his head. "Someone else on our side did it. You and the others were our last hope and could not be risked. The body has been a deterrent."

"What of Burditt and Matiu?"

Vilks shrugged. "There is no way to know. Your team was the last one still working. The others have long been eliminated within the system. Please tell me you had found something."

She shrugged. "We were close, but they need me. We found a weakness but its botanical." She lied.

"Your specialty," he replied. "You can't log in for very long. There's no food."

"Doesn't matter, it needs to be done."

Before she could pull the glasses back into place and plug in the commander grabbed her hand. "Faith's last words were Wolf in Sheep's Clothing. Does that make sense?"

She nodded and keyed her ID in. The program had

continued running and she found herself in the infinity lab. Matiu sat alone at a computer staring blankly at her.

"You're back?"

She nodded.

He let out a long sigh letting his shoulders sagged. "You and Burditt logged off within minutes of each other. I've been trying to work out a solution, but I don't know this stuff."

"Fortress has fallen. I don't know how much time I have."

Matiu ran his hands through his hair. "The last message from Delsin was that they were tearing the rock off Tower. We haven't much time."

She sat down and started working out the proportions. "Do you know how long we've been here?" she asked as she worked.

"A week tops. The diet stream sends warning if it's any longer."

Juliet shook her head. "Three months. Vilks has been refilling mine and he yanked me because Fortress is out of supply. Faith was taken out because she was drawing too much attention."

Matiu's eyes widened. "You saw Faith?"

She nodded.

"Good, I had worried they had sent a feedback loop on her. We thought the same for you. Burditt received a message from his De/Su officers and had to log. He said not to worry that he would find us."

Juliet decided against telling Matiu about Faith, and concentrated on her work. "Did the information I found in the egg transfer to you?"

Matiu nodded. "It was exactly what we needed, but you're not going to like it."

"What do you mean? It didn't show the origin of the threat?"

Matiu pressed a finger to his lips and tapped away at the console. A moment later the Unit 6 image was barricaded by a stream of code that encircled it. "I didn't say that," coughed Matiu. "It was like we figured before the safety net; the threat is not external as the good Commander wants us to believe."

"What?"

"The Educators and De/Su are working together to bring down the Sanctuaries and I can't figure out why."

Juliet shook her head. "Wolves in sheep's clothing."

Matiu arched an eyebrow. "What?"

"Faith wanted us to know about a wolf in sheep's clothing. If it is the De/Su in charge then Vilks has set it all up. We can't give them what they want."

"We have no choice. We don't know what will happen when

this stuff is released, but if it doesn't happen, the Sanctuaries will be torn apart from within." He reached a hand out to her. "Have you finished?"

She nodded and handed him the equation. "For better or worse."

He swallowed hard, his Adam's apple quivering. "For better or worse," he said and pressed the key to transmit the formula to Delsin.

The room flashed yellow and everything went black.

Screams were the first thing to rouse Juliet from her sleep. She opened her eyes but all she saw was blackness around her. She could not move her arms and a thick strap bound her chest against a cushioned board. The faint piney scent of Thryptomene infiltrated her nose and lungs. There was another scent beneath it, something she could not identify. With each breath she felt more alive.

A humming sound came from the darkness and the belts around her loosened. She slid her wrists out of their holders and tried to bring them up. She pressed her hands against a metal wall directly in front of her. Plastic tubes lay cold against her skin and she tried to pull them out, but they burned as the slid out of her veins.

"Stop," a familiar voice called from the other side of the metal.

"Burditt?" she whimpered.

"Yes, wait a moment, we're working on opening the pod. Stay still!" he commanded.

A sliver of light formed a ring around her from head to foot. A scraping sound followed as the metal wall was pulled away from her and Burditt stood before her in a grey coverall. He was thin, lacking all the muscle of a soldier. Beside him was Matiu, who was much shorter than his simulated self.

"How did you get to Fortress?" she asked, her voice catching in her throat.

"This isn't Fortress," Matiu replied.

Burditt stepped forward and began removing the bindings on her legs. He looked up at her. "This is reality."

Vliks stepped out of the shadows. "Correct. Thanks to you, the second program has been broken and we can now live outside the Program."

"The threat was a ruse, we weren't ending an enemy we were waking ourselves," whispered Burditt as he pulled off the last band that was around her neck, his lips brushing her ear. "It was all a lie."

"Now we will face reality the way we were intended! Not

hooked up to machine living in a pixelated database!" preened Vilks. He turned away from them and started down the pod-lined corridor. "Come children! Let us finish waking the rest." The commander began placing marks on the pods as he went along.

"We found the wolf in sheep's clothing," muttered Matiu, who turned on his heel to follow Commander Vilks.

Juliet leaned into Burditt, looking over his shoulder at the departing pair and the rows upon rows of black pods lining the hall. "We face reality now, for better or worse."

About Andrea L. Staum

Andrea L. Staum is the author of *Blood of the Sire* Book 1 of the *Dragonchild Lore* series. She's a trained motorcycle technician with an Associates in Supervisory Management, is an amateur home renovator, and somehow manages to find time to write. She lives in south central Wisconsin with her husband, two demanding cats, and two ornery rabbits. Please visit her Facebook page at: facebook.com/pages/Andrea-L-Staum-Author/146878242143910

Mr. Trueworthy

by Carol Smallwood

Once upon a time, an insurance services representative lived in a decaying stone mansion by a pond far from the road near Traverse City. His ad in the Yellow Pages read:

Trueworthy's Allstate Insurance Agency Has Been Meeting
Traverse City Needs Since 1970
Free, red custom-made, genuine alligator-like skin wallets with
each new policy!
Auto, Farm, Life, Homeowners. Affordable payment plans.
Competitive Rates.

Since his work mostly involved investment counseling with a lot of work on-line, he was seldom seen. Dogs nearing his high iron fence (kept in good repair) would slink away with lowered heads and hair raised on their backs. The raccoons did not even try to get near the frogs in the pond. There should have been many butterflies and moths attracted to the pond, but there were none and so there were no birds.

Neighborhood children called him Yeller Hammer. After one boy who'd seen him hammering said, "He yelled a lot and took a shot at me," kids stopped going there at Halloween.

The rich man lived by himself because his wife disappeared after their children left home. He spent many hours each day thinking how to cheat even more people so he could get richer. When the moon was full he would take his gun to the pond, shoot frogs on lily pads and hammer them thin on the rocks to get the most skin. He used their skin to make the "free, custom-made, genuine alligator-like skin bags with each new policy" as seen in his ad.

One year when the maples were turning to scarlet and gold, the man noticed all the frogs gathered at one end of the pond where the rocks were. The next few days he noticed the lily pads kept coming closer to the edge of the pond.

The next night he began hearing noises from his cellar that sounded like "plop, plop" but he thought it was water dripping. The next night the frogs began croaking, greedycreep, greedycreep, greedycreep, in the cellar and soon the croaking lasted day and night.

When the croaking got so loud he couldn't hear stockbrokers on the telephone, he asked his closest neighbor half a mile away to come and asked: "Do you hear frogs croaking?"

"No, Mr. Trueworthy, I hear nothing." As the neighbor was entering the decaying stone mansion, he remembered the day the investor had cheated him on a policy.

"Come and stand by this floor register so you can hear better."

"No, Mr. Trueworthy, I hear nothing." He remembered the day the investor had spread lies about him.

"Bend over the register so you can hear better."

"No, Mr. Trueworthy, I hear nothing. As he bent over he had remembered the day when he had stolen his mail.

The next day the croaking became louder. Greedycreep, greedycreep, greedycreep

He asked his neighbor's son: "Do you hear frogs croaking?"

"No, Mr. Trueworthy, I hear nothing." As the neighbor's son was entering the decaying stone mansion, he remembered the day the investor shot his dog and left it to die.

"Come and stand by this floor register so you can hear better."

"No, Mr. Trueworthy, I hear nothing." He remembered the day the investor refused to reimburse him when his motorcycle was stolen.

"Bend over the register so you can hear better."

"No, Mr. Trueworthy, I hear nothing. As he bent over he had remembered the day when he'd gone back on his word to help sponsor his soccer team.

The rich man stuffed rags in his ears to block out the croaking. He saved all his Seagram's to drink at night so he could sleep and his voice became more cracked each night yelling (he didn't want to spend money for pest control service) to scare the frogs away. The chorus of, *greedycreep, greedycreep, greedycreep*, became louder and louder each day.

One day when Mr. Trueworthy was repairing his high iron

151

fence dressed in a tattered tee-shirt displaying, "A Penny Saved is a Penny Earned," he heard the weeds rustling behind him. He whirled around with his hammer raised.

A large frog hopped up to him quaking. "Please, sir, do not kill my wife."

"I do not kill."

A smaller frog hopped up to him shaking. "Please, sir, do not kill my daughter."

"I do not kill."

A tiny frog hopped up to him quaking and shaking. "Please, sir, do not kill my brother."

"I do not kill."

It was at the height of fall colors when ducks were flying south in "V" formation and brown cat tails were becoming fuzzy when a United States Department of Agriculture Natural Resources Planner called the authorities about Mr. Trueworthy. The planner had been checking on a tree disease Mr. Trueworthy refused to treat which was spreading in the neighborhood. He told the sheriff no one came to the front door three days in a row and thought the man might be ill.

When the sheriff and deputy sheriff came, they couldn't find any sign of the man inside the decaying stone mansion but noticed a narrow path of newly crushed weeds from the pond to the cellar door. The deputy sheriff saw some red lily pads and tufts of white but thought they were fall colors and milkweed puffs. The sheriff spotted yellow teeth near the cellar door but thought they were from a wild animal and that the yellow nails were dried weeds. The tattered tee-shirt (they could just make out the word "Penny") was thought to be from some farmer's scarecrow.

The men stayed close to each other after finding Mr. Trueworthy's bumper sticker, "Support Your Right to Bear Arms," impaled on his high iron fence. There was an odd smell in the air and each noticed the other quaking and shaking. They kept looking over their shoulders and were glad to leave the decaying stone mansion as quickly as they could. The sheriff and his deputy were so eager to leave, they missed seeing the frogs hopping down the narrow path of newly crushed weeds. And the diving boards in the pond in the shape of human ribs.

Before he got into his car the deputy sheriff asked, "Have you ever heard such a loud bunch of frogs?"

The sheriff shook his head. "You could almost believe they were having some sort of a celebration, couldn't you?"

When they were having coffee at McDonald's the sheriff remarked, "You know, I can't get the sound of those croaking frogs out of my head." After taking aspirin with a third cup of coffee, he said, "Let's go and write up our report."

The deputy rose and hitched up his belt. He was still shaking and quaking. He picked up his "free, custom-made, genuine alligator-like skin wallet" from the table and remarked, "You know, I can still smell that odd smell."

The decaying stone mansion was soon said to be haunted because hammering could be heard again on moonlit nights. If anyone had the courage to investigate they'd have noticed the lily pads displaying fresh (pounded extra thin) pink skin formed a smiley face in the pond.

Carol Smallwood's over four dozen books include *Women on Poetry: Writing, Revising, Publishing and Teaching* on Poets & Writers Magazine list of Best Books for Writers; *Women Writing on Family: Tips on Writing, Teaching and Publishing* (Key Publishing House, 2012); *Lily's Odyssey* (All Things That Matter Press, 2010).

You can find out more about her here: pw.org/content/carol_smallwood

Iron Henry

By Kasidy Manisco

It wasn't the first time Adam bled for his job. It wouldn't be the last. Adam wiped his hands on a dirty handkerchief and stuck it back in his pocket, trying to concentrate for the last few minutes of his shift on a gear that wouldn't stick right. He tried his hardest, but the gear wouldn't go where it was supposed to, and the nuts wouldn't line up right. He sighed, frustrated, and tried one more time, but it wouldn't fit on the short rod sticking out of the bottom of the machine, and Adam scraped his already raw fingers on a sharp point and cut his finger. He automatically stuck the finger in his mouth, then quickly wiped the blood and spit away on his handkerchief before stowing it away again.

Adam frowned. The stupid machine wouldn't work if the gear wasn't fixed, and if the gear wasn't fixed, no product on this machine would be made, and then the workers wouldn't be paid. It was something his boss liked to call a "shit problem".

Well, Adam was right vexed. He let the wrench fall from his stained and dirty fingers to clank on the cement floor and looked around the big room. It was one big room that was full of other machines, flat on top with rollers constantly moving back and forth as they attempted to make paper. Except for the machine Adam worked on, anyway. He took his cap off and scratched his thick hair, as if he were taking a short break, not that he could really be seen doing so. Still, he had to make sure no one was watching.

There were very few people working today, like any day. People were quickly being replaced, and only a few—mostly women and children—were working, not that people were happy about it. But you had to do what you had to do.

So, when Adam saw no one looking his way, he hunched over the gear and frowned in intense concentration. He could feel his mind work, could feel something move as he worked his brain in ways a normal human wouldn't dare dream of. Adam moved the gear with his mind, his brain pushing the gear that extra inch, then aligning the nuts and screws. He screwed it all in, using nothing but his mind. Oh, he used his hands to help hold the screws in place, but it was just for show, so no one would see him just sitting there and come over to investigate.

When he was done, he sat back on his heels, wiped the sweat that had popped out on his forehead and smirked. Well, how about that? It wasn't easy, doing what he did, but damn if it wasn't satisfying. Except for when his head started to pound, of course, but that was par for the course. You couldn't do what he did without any sort of consequences.

Still, Adam thought, rising and wiping his hands again, and bent for the wrench and screw driver, sometimes nothing would do except hard work. Something he wished his little brother would learn someday. In the very near future.

His shift finally over, Adam grabbed the book he generally hid under the machines when he was working—either fixing old machines or making new ones since the company couldn't afford to buy them elsewhere—and stuffed it beneath his grubby shirt and the waistband of his pants. Then he put his tools away, grabbed his bit of coin, and walked out of the only door on the first floor.

Adam didn't mind the work, not really. It was a bit on the boring side, not to mention exhausting, but it kept food on the table, and it kept them from living on the streets. He tried to study when he could, and tried to force knowledge into his far more excitable brother. Adam kept telling his brother that if he wanted something better, he had to get some learning in him, but Henry never listened, and Adam didn't know how to make him, other than to tie him to a chair. Satisfying, perhaps, but it wouldn't make his attention any more focused. Sighing, Adam slumped against the wall of a nearby building, just to catch his breath for a minute. Adam was only fifteen, but already he had become a parent to a ten year old, overactive child.

When Adam felt he was ready, he stretched, wiped his hands on his coveralls, and patted his pocket, feeling a small smile creep onto his face as he walked down the sidewalk. Today was payday, and he'd been given just enough money to buy his little brother a treat on his way to pick him up. Adam had to admit that he was lucky—lucky enough to have persuaded his boss, Stan, to allow him to work for him instead of another woman. Lucky that neither he nor Henry had to work as a chimney sweep.

Adam, feeling strangely lighthearted for such a long day of work, walked away from the gigantic factory building, and made his way towards the city center, where the shops were. Once there, he dodged people in a hurry, jumped out of the way of horses and their carriages, and kept his right hand in his pocket to avoid any grimy little cutpurses. He'd seen them at work, had been one of them once upon a time. He knew how good some of them were. And he couldn't afford for them to take his hard earned money. Not just for himself, or to keep food on the table, but as an example to his brother. The kid needed to know that hard work did indeed pay off, that as hard as he worked now, someday it would culminate in success. His brother didn't believe him, but Adam had to be a good example anyway. Someone had to show the kid the ropes, show him how to be a real man. Unfortunately, Adam was it. The only one.

Sometimes he resented it. He was supposed to be in school, supposed to live his own life, not put it on hold. Adam had dreams; he wanted to search for his purpose. But life didn't always work out the way you wanted. And he would rather this life than a life without his brother.

At the market Adam bought Henry his favorite treat, and tucked it safely away in his other pocket. Henry had been good this week, and he deserved a little something to remind him that being good reaped rewards.

Errand done, he hurried towards the sewing factory, where his brother waited. The factory was a great deal smaller than the one Adam worked at, but it was still a big stone slab of a building, with upwards of seven stories. The windows were clouded over with smog from the machines that were taking over their world, and the brick was just as dirty and sooty as everything else in London.

As Adam reached the building where his brother worked, a cloud passed over him and he shivered and rubbed his arms.

Adam looked with dread at the shadowy spot where Henry should have been waiting. He was conspicuously not there, the shadows taking up space where a boy half his height should be. Adam's mouth firmed as he tried to reassure himself that Henry hadn't been snatched.

That damn kid, he thought. He never listens. If he had been listening, he'd be sitting there, or standing, fidgeting and getting his clothes, which Adam painstakingly fixed every other day after a long day of work, all dirty and ripped up. He couldn't entirely blame his brother, as even he would find sitting at a little machine all day torturous, but Henry knew what it was like on these streets, especially when it grew dark.

He thought back to when he saw Henry after a year away for school, crouching on a street corner, filthy, hungry, alone. Adam didn't want that to happen to him again.

Adam forced his heart to stop galloping in his chest so he could think. All right, if Henry were of his own mind, and not snatched, where would he go? Not far, because even Henry would not be so stupid, and he wouldn't want to worry Adam. At least the boy had something of a conscience, even if he refused to use it sometimes.

Taking a deep breath, Adam circled the square building in a jog, taking in the deserted places, the shadowed spaces, until he came back to the same spot, right outside the front door. Nothing.

No, Henry must be running around somewhere, oblivious as usual. There couldn't be another option.

Adam wouldn't accept it.

What would entertain a ten year old boy? He thought, becoming frantic and angry. He ought to know this. Adam turned around and looked at the other similar buildings around him. Nothing that would attract a ten year old.

And then he spotted it. Stairs climbed the wall on one side of the building across from him, which stopped about a floor under the roof. A ladder was connected to it, which led straight to the roof, which was flat and open. Perfect.

Jaw tight, Adam ran over to the stairs and climbed them. Sure enough, at the top Henry stood on the far side, standing right on top of the ledge. His arms were thrown wide, his feet spread, the tips of his shoes hanging just over the edge. Adam's heart took a dive past his toes.

"Henry!" he yelled, scrambling up and over the ledge and racing to his little brother. Once he got there he would strangle the idiot.

Henry turned to him, seeming unconcerned. He smiled and waved, bouncing on his toes, saying, "Hallo, Adam! Look at what I'm doing!"

Adam, in no mood for Henry's games, grabbed him by his grubby shirt and yanked him off the ledge. He tried not to imagine what would have happened had Henry fallen, tried not to picture what he would look like lying there on the cold cement, broken and bloody. Dead.

Heart pounding, Adam shook Henry. "What the devil is wrong with you?" he shouted, the wind whipping his words away. Lord Almighty, if anything had happened to that fool boy...it wasn't something Adam could accept.

Henry, looking so young with his baby face and his long hair falling into his eyes, the brave, fearless Henry for once looked uncertain. "Adam?" he asked, almost hesitantly. His brother was not shy, or hesitant. He rushed headlong into whatever sort of danger or adventure he could find, and he was always sorry for it afterwards, for worrying Adam. But Adam was sorry too, sorry every day that he realized Henry had been alone, and he knew sorry just didn't cut it.

Adam gritted his teeth. "You could have fallen, do you realize that? You could have died!" Logic wouldn't work on Henry—he simply didn't care. Perhaps Adam was being disingenuous. Henry did care, to a point. He just didn't care about the risk to his own life.

"But it was fun, and I was bored sitting in that chair all day. I hate staring at a sewing machine. And besides, I wouldn't have fallen. I have good balance." But Henry suddenly looked unsure.

"But you might have fallen," Adam insisted. "You would have left me alone and it'd hurt me, do you realize that?"

That, Henry understood. He looked down, solemn and still in Adam's hands. "I'm sorry. I didn't mean to scare you. But you were late and I was just so *bored*."

Adam's anger and worry dissipated. He couldn't stay mad at the little bugger. And that was the worst part.

Letting go of Henry's shirt with difficulty, he sighed and pulled out Henry's treat. "I bought this for you."

Henry's dark eyes lit up and a grin split his face. "For me?"

Adam lifted a finger and said, "Only if you don't do this again. Promise me." But Henry wasn't listening, already distracted, so he grabbed the boy's chin and forced his little brother to look at him. "Promise me."

Henry took exactly two seconds to think about it, nod, then snatch the treat away from Adam's fingers. Adam sighed. Well, he supposed that was better than nothing. He grabbed his squirrelly brother before he could move too far away and rubbed his knuckles into his ratty blond hair, using the move as an excuse to hug his brother, to feel him breathing, laughing.

Henry squirmed away from him. He didn't need his big brother to watch over him so closely. It broke Adam's heart a little, though in all honesty he was glad Henry was around to annoy him. Even if he hated it.

"Hey, Adam, look, no hands!" Henry yelled on his way down the rickety ladder.

Frustration burst out of Adam in one bellow. "Henry!"

After he'd chased Henry and wrestled him by Adam's side, they stopped by their parents' graves to leave a single flower, a simple reminder that they had been loved. Adam could admit to himself now that he'd taken his parents for granted. He'd used what little money they had to go off to school, because he wanted to do something, be something great. His parents had let him take the money, but Adam still felt guilty. Thought, perhaps, that maybe, if he hadn't taken the money, if he'd stayed, his mother wouldn't have gotten sick and died, and his father wouldn't have died in the mines a few months later. Leaving eight-year-old Henry alone, until one of his old friends spotted Henry squatting on a street corner, filthy and emaciated, and sent him a letter.

A Goddamned letter.

That was when Adam realized that family was more important than greatness. But it was a lesson learned too late.

Adam patted Henry's head, and he looked up at Adam with such love and trust. Adam smiled and said, "Let's go home."

Shadows blanketed them as they walked down the alley on their way home later that night. The place was usually deserted, but it was later than usual. Their normal route had been blocked by construction, so they had had to go around, and now it was getting darker, and Adam felt more anxious. He knew what the streets were like at night, and he didn't want to take a chance. Not with Henry.

It turned out his efforts made no difference.

A solitary man appeared at the far end of the alley. He stood with his arms crossed, legs spread wide. The man's face was mostly obscured by shadows, but Adam caught a hint of a smile. Adam grabbed Henry's shoulder, his fingers like pincers. Henry saw what his older brother saw, and stopped, backing up into Adam, who palmed his dead father's knife in a sweaty hand. He began backing away slowly, Henry huddling close by his side.

Two more men stood at the other end of the alley behind them, and Adam knew they didn't stand a chance. But that didn't mean he wouldn't fight. He'd given up once. Never again.

Lord be with us, Adam pleaded.

"Hey there, boy," one of the men called out as the three men began strolling closer.

"You look lost," the one behind Adam said. It forced Adam to look at him, to notice his beefy arms and his confident stride, to smell the liquor on his breath and to see his dirty, rotten teeth. Adam turned sideways so he could see all three men. He moved Henry behind him, so Henry's back was against the wall of one of the buildings. For once, he listened and stayed there.

"We're not lost," Adam said. His voice sounded confident, strong, but Adam felt anything but.

"Wasn't a suggestion, boy." Adam had no clue which one of them spoke. "You're lost. We can help you with that."

"No," Adam forced out. He brandished his blade in front of him, sweeping it from one side to the other. Adam was more of an intellectual than a fighter, but he'd read how fights were done.

"Look," Adam said, digging out the precious coins he'd earned, the ones that would have given them food for the next day or two. He held them out to the man nearest him on his right. "Here are a few coins. Take them. It's all I have."

The man, who was thinner than the other two, smirked and reached out slowly to grab the coins, as if he were prolonging the torture. Adam watched his hard earned money go to someone else, and it made him angry. Here he was, trying to teach his brother the value of hard work, and these older, hardened men—scum, all of them—who should know better were just taking it away, as if it meant nothing.

"Please, let us go. We have nothing else." Adam didn't quite beg, but he came close. He may have had the knife, but he knew damn well these men held the upper hand.

Suddenly the lone man on his left snatched Henry away from him by his shirt. Adam's hand shot out, but he missed, and the man dragged Henry a few feet away kicking and screaming.

"Whoa there," the man said appreciatively. "The boy's got grit. Unlike you." A grin widened on his face, showing off his unhealthy teeth as he glanced down at Henry's feet. "Well would you look at that. Little un's got some nice shoes there. My boy needs new shoes."

"Just let him go! You can have the shoes, just let him go!" Adam lunged, but the other two men wrapped their arms around him and yanked him back. One grabbed his head, his cap falling clean off. He struggled, but their grip was too strong. The man on his right knocked the knife out of his hand.

The one who held Henry laughed as he yelled and kicked and punched. Henry was still small for his age, and nothing made an impact. "Well, I reckon I'll get them anyway." And he lifted Henry over his shoulder and walked away.

He *walked away*. With Henry.

"No!" Adam yelled, panic and fear twining around his heart and spreading through his limbs. No, he couldn't lose Henry. Not again. He'd promised Henry he would keep him safe. Adam couldn't break that promise.

He jumped in the men's grip, but their fingers tightened hard enough to bruise.

The two men laughed at his struggles, and one bent to pick up his knife. Adam watched, stricken, feeling his face freeze. They were going to kill him and Henry both. Just for a few coins and a pair of shoes. And he would have failed Henry. Again. The thought fueled Adam's anger, stoking the fire until it blazed with heat. The extra something in his mind flexed, and then there was a cacophony of sharp cracks.

The man's fingers broke one bone at a time.

He bellowed, grabbing his hand and falling to his knees, hunching over his broken fingers. Adam felt a fierce triumph even though fear made him sick. His ability wasn't strong enough to do that, and yet he had used it that way. The second man stared for a second before yanking his head back by his dark hair. The man's fingers dug into Adam's scalp, and Adam shoved backward, using his ability to again break a man's fingers. The man yowled and let go, falling back, hunching over his hands, body bowed almost in penitence.

The other man was recovering, and as Adam reached for his knife, he jabbed with a claw-like hand. Adam jumped but was still scored by the claws, and he slashed out with the knife, catching the man's cheekbone. The slice went all the way up to his eye. Blood poured out of the deep cut, and the man groaned, placing his good hand over the wound. Adam should have broken both hands on this one. Something wet fell on his upper lip and Adam realized it was blood.

A scream rent the air and Adam whipped around. It was a child's scream, pure and high-pitched. Terrified.

Henry.

Adam sprinted down the alley and outside it, but he stopped, looking around him frantically. *Where is he, where is he?* Adam chanted to himself. Empty buildings surrounded him. No way to know where they went.

Adam's eyes darted around. There, on his right. A door stood open, when it should have been closed, locked. A terrible thought gripped him. He knew what that building housed.

Adam ran, blind to anything but that door and the shadows that lay inside. He lit a gaslamp and searched the big room with his eyes, calling Henry's name. The inside was a metal forest, long beams reaching up into the ceiling, trying to puncture it to merge with the clouds and the air outside, while other pieces lay scattered along the floor, next to giant machines still only halfway through creation. Some pieces had been left on the ground, broken or warped or burned, casualties of a new iron-working world.

And in that rubble he found Henry.

"Henry!" he screamed, running to fall at Henry's side. His shoes were gone, the bastard, and a short, thin piece of metal as long as Adam's forearm had been rammed through his heart.

"Henry," he pleaded, picking him up and holding him in his arms. Tears crested, fell. "Henry, say something."

He expected silence, but his brother coughed and he blinked, too slowly. His glazed eyes searched out Adam's face and he smiled weakly. "Hallo, Adam," he said, before he coughed again.

Blood spilled out of his mouth, and his eyes widened in fear.

"Shh, it's okay," Adam said, cradling Henry's head against his chest. "It's just a little blood." He swallowed, tried not to let his voice crack. He looked around, searching for the man, but he was gone. All Adam had left was a dying brother without his shoes.

Adam had failed his brother.

"Adam," Henry said, his voice weaker than before.

"Yes, Henry?" he asked, just as softly.

"Can I have some more sweets when we get home?"

Adam laughed, choked on a sob. Such a simple request. He decided it was okay this time to lie.

"Of course, peanut," he said, using the name their ma had always called him. "You can have all the sweets you want." Adam petted Henry's thick blond hair, which had begun to curl at the ends. He had their mother's hair, her looks. Adam was stuck looking like their father, the big brute, but anyone could tell from their eyes, the shape of their noses, that they were brothers.

Adam swallowed and clumsily stood, hugging a limp Henry to his chest. He had to try to save his brother. He didn't know how he was going to do it—the closest doctor was several miles away—but he had to. He couldn't lose Henry too.

"Perhaps I can be of help," a voice said behind him.

Adam turned around to see an old woman. She wore a long dress, though not dirty, and she wore her silver hair in a long braid down her back. She was bony rather than plump, and while she had wrinkles around her eyes and her mouth, her face was baby-faced, a little like Henry. Her eyes held an ageless quality and yet they seemed to have known many more years than a human being should. Prickles ran down Adam's arms as he stared at this modest-looking woman with the kind, thin-lipped smile and the sharp eagle eyes. Shadows seemed to cling to her, like the rest of this place, the lone gaslamp casting hardly enough light to see by.

"Who are you?" Adam asked quietly. He wanted his tone to be stronger, more demanding, but his mother had taught him to show respect towards his elders, and the lesson was ingrained deep.

Instead of answering, she leaned forward, the better to see Henry. "Your brother is dying rather quickly. The shaking has stopped, do you see?"

Adam didn't see, because he didn't dare tear his gaze away from the woman, but he could feel it. Henry's skin was cold, clammy, his little body too still for a boy always in motion.

"Tell me, little prince, will you do anything for your brother?" she asked, her head tilting with curiosity.

What the devil?

"Are you saying you can save him?" Adam asked, clutching Henry to his chest.

One delicate eyebrow rose. "Answer my question, little prince." Her accent was strange, and her voice made shivers crawl down his spine, but if she could save Henry, he could ignore the rest.

"Yes," Adam said without hesitation. "But I'm no prince."

The woman tilted her head. "We shall see." She stepped forward, walking around Adam to stand in front of Henry. She knelt down and passed her hand over Henry from head to foot. Adam didn't know what the woman had done, but Henry's eyes closed, his gasps eased into shallow breaths and he stopped moving, as if entirely dead.

"What have you done?" Adam asked, panicked.

"Be easy. Your brother is in stasis. I have bought us a few extra minutes."

"Are you...a witch?" Adam asked, almost skeptically. Perhaps not a witch, he thought as he calmed a little, but someone like him.

The woman smiled faintly, amused, as if she could read his thoughts. Oh Lord, what if she *could* read his thoughts?

"Time is wasting, little prince. If I save your brother, will you do anything I say?"

"Anything you say?" Adam asked. He felt as if he were under water, that everything was coming to him too slowly.

"Will you be my servant, Adam Price, for the life of your brother?" she asked patiently.

Adam hesitated. What was this? Was this even real? Or was it a dream? Adam's head might have been filled with cotton for all the thoughts his mind managed to cling to.

She glanced down, studying Henry with an analytical gaze. "Your brother will expire within the next few minutes. Even my powers cannot defy death. Make your decision, quickly."

Adam heard the clock winding down on his brother's life. He opened his mouth, closed it, then shouted, "Yes! Yes, okay, I'll be your servant. I'll do whatever you want, just don't let him die."

"And you will keep your word?" she asked, watching him through narrowed eyes.

"Yes. Yes, I will keep my word."

Her lips pulled up into the smallest of smiles and time suddenly sped up again. Adam's pulse thrummed and his cheeks flushed from the anticipation, the anxiety.

The woman looked down, a long finger tapping her lips. "Yes, this piece will do. However, I need something more."

"Anything," Adam said.

"Find me a few small, thin, flat metal pieces, if you please. And do hurry. We have precious few minutes left."

Adam set Henry gently on the floor. Then he ran.

He searched the first floor frantically. Everything he found was too big, too bulky, the iron used to build machines, not fix hearts. Despair bit Adam hard when he couldn't find the right pieces, but then he turned around, and there they were, two pieces of flat metal just waiting for him to take them. He snatched them up and sprinted back to the witch. Back to Henry.

"I have them," he choked out, waving the two pieces of metal in front of her.

She pushed his hand away with an expression of irritation on her face. "Yes, yes, now hold them here and here," she said, pointing.

Adam looked down and his jaw fell open in horror. What the devil had she done? His brother's chest had been ripped open, revealing Henry's heart. The rod had been removed and cut into three pieces, which sat to the side. Adam was frozen, stuck between anguish and rage, until he realized that there was no blood. Except Henry's skin had been peeled back. Adam could see Henry's ribcage, his heart and lungs. How could there be no blood?

"Now, if you please," the witch said, steel in her tone. "Unless you want your brother to die."

Adam wanted to stop, to demand some sort of explanation, but he couldn't risk it, couldn't risk Henry's life on his questions. Swallowing down his fear, he knelt and did as she commanded, placing the metal pieces where she directed. A few seconds passed, and Adam tried not to acknowledge that he literally held his brother's heart in his hands. He tried to ignore how the heart felt, how squishy and small it seemed. And then, right before Adam's eyes, the metal sank a little, and the ragged, torn remains of the heart, connected to them, meshing with them. The metal became almost fluid and transformed, looking and feeling more natural. The color didn't change. Henry's heart looked like a patchwork quilt, the kind his ma used to make before she died.

"And now for the final touch," the witch murmured, and the rod that had been used to take Henry's life...now saved it. She took each metal rod and it became like putty in her hands, as she wrapped each piece around his heart. Three iron bands flowed around Henry's heart, strengthening it even more. The bands remained a bit thick, but in a moment, Henry's heart started beating again the way it should.

"The iron will not restrict him in any way," the witch said, sounding pleased. Adam couldn't stop staring at the beating heart. It was...beautiful.

The witch waved a hand and Henry's skin flowed back over his chest, becoming smooth and unblemished again. The shirt was ruined, but Adam didn't care. The stasis had worn off, and Henry breathed normally, as if he were asleep. Adam placed a tentative hand on his chest, just to make sure. The partially artificial heart beat strong beneath his hand and Adam wanted to cry like a baby.

Henry would be okay. Adam hadn't failed him after all.

The witch stood. "Now," she said, "you will come with me."

"What?" Adam asked and jumped to his feet, even though his whole body ached. "What do you mean?"

The witch stood there, her hands folded in front of her, with a stern expression. "You promised to be my servant, did you not?"

"Of course, mum," Adam said.

"Then as my servant, I require you to come with me."

And leave Henry? Alone? His mind flashed back to that dirty boy on the street. "Wait. I—I want to make another deal."

The woman tilted her head, her interest piqued. "Oh?"

"Please, I don't want to leave Henry alone. I'll do whatever you want, just let me be with him. He needs me."

He could see her considering it, could see the cogs turning in her eyes. "That too will cost you," she said slowly.

Adam nodded. "I know."

"You say you are not a prince," she said after another quiet moment. "But you would sacrifice yourself for your brother. Is that not princely?" Her mouth tilted up in amusement, but Adam couldn't see what was so damned funny. "I accept your terms, little prince."

She stepped forward and pressed a kiss to his forehead. It was cold, slimy, and Adam instantly jerked away. But the feeling spread from his forehead to his torso, limbs, his legs and feet. Adam's vision went black, and when he opened his eyes again, everything looked different, felt different. He bounced and realized that the witch carried him as she walked. Walked away from Henry.

Adam realized too, that he had been turned into a bloody frog.

"We," the witch said as she strolled down the dark street, "are going to do great things together. Do not worry. You shall see your brother again someday, of that I am certain."

Adam laughed, but it only came out as a hoarse croak. That was all he'd ever wanted, why he'd gone away to school, so he could learn and do great things. Only now he couldn't care less about it. He only cared about Henry.

Adam couldn't help but feel that he had failed Henry, for good this time. *I'm sorry*, he tried to tell Henry. And then he heard a response. It wasn't words, but he could feel Henry's reaction, his surprise and fear. And that's when he knew everything was going to be okay. Adam wouldn't be able to be there for Henry like he wanted. Wouldn't be able to get Henry out of trouble, wouldn't be able to do too many of the things an older brother should do, but he could still be a good influence on him, and be there in his thoughts if not in body. It wasn't what he wanted, but it would have to be enough, until they could find each other again.

It would be difficult, just like learning to be a parent had been difficult, but they would both manage. They could do nothing else.

Get up, Henry, he said, and for a second, he could see through his brother's eyes, see the darkened building and the imposing metal all around him. Henry rose shakily, and the world tilted. Henry didn't like the building. Adam didn't think he could remember what had happened to him, but he felt it when Henry rubbed his chest.

Go home, peanut. It'll be okay. It's safe there. Adam had no idea if that would be the case, but he knew Henry couldn't stay there.

For once, Henry listened to him, and left on unsteady feet to find home, and when he arrived, Adam breathed a sigh of relief, though it sounded odd coming from his new frog throat. Henry was safe. Adam lost Henry's sight then, but he could still feel the connection between them, strong. Unbreakable.

Warmth spread through him, and anguish. He felt his brother's fear in his mind. *It'll be okay, Henry. I'm with you. Always.* Henry couldn't respond, or if he did, Adam didn't hear it, but it didn't matter, because *Henry* could hear *him.*

They were brothers. Adam might be a frog and Henry might have an iron heart, but they were, in a strange way, together. And because of that, Adam knew it would be okay.

About Kasidy Manisco

Kasidy Manisco holds two Bachelor's degrees, one in English and one in Secondary Education, and a Master's degree in English. Currently she works at a library. In her spare time she writes as much as she can, reads everything she can get her hands on, and spends time with family. She is currently working on an adult urban fantasy novel and a young adult urban fantasy novel, with a few short stories thrown in to the mix. She lives with her hyper dog and two cats who love to make life interesting.